FRIENDS for a SEASON

RED VELVET

Sandra Byrd

BETHANYHOUSE
MINNEAPOLIS, MINNESOTA

Red Velvet
Copyright © 2005
Sandra Byrd

Cover design by Melinda Schumacher

Unless otherwise identified, Scripture quotations are from the HOLY BIBLE, NEW INTERNATIONAL VERSION®. Copyright © 1973, 1978, 1984 by International Bible Society. Used by permission of Zondervan Publishing House. All rights reserved.

Scripture quotations identified The Message are from *The Message*. Copyright © 1993, 1994, 1995 by Eugene H. Peterson. Used by permission of NavPress Publishing Group.

Scripture quotations in chapter 7 are from the *Holy Bible*, New Living Translation, copyright © 1996. Used by permission of Tyndale House Publishers, Inc., Wheaton, Illinois 60189. All rights reserved.

All rights reserved. No part of this publication may be reproduced, stored in a retrieval system, or transmitted in any form or by any means—electronic, mechanical, photocopying, recording, or otherwise—without the prior written permission of the publisher and copyright owners.

Published by Bethany House Publishers
11400 Hampshire Avenue South
Bloomington, Minnesota 55438

Bethany House Publishers is a division of
Baker Publishing Group, Grand Rapids, Michigan.

Printed in the United States of America

Library of Congress Cataloging-in-Publication Data

Byrd, Sandra.
    Red velvet / Sandra Byrd.
        p. cm. — (Friends for a season)
        Summary: While comforting her mother after chemotherapy treatments, fourteen-year-old Quinn reads her parent's teen-years diary and determines to help her mother accomplish some forgotten goals.
        ISBN 0-7642-0022-4 (pbk.)
        [1. Cancer—Fiction. 2. Mothers and daughters—Fiction. 3. Christian life—Fiction. 4. Family life—Fiction.] I. Title. II. Series.
    PZ7.B9898Red   2005
    [Fic]—dc22   2005020518

RED VELVET

Books by
Sandra Byrd
FROM BETHANY HOUSE PUBLISHERS

Girl Talk
Chatting With Girls Like You
A Growing-Up Guide
The Inside-Out Beauty Book

FRIENDS FOR A SEASON
Island Girl
Chopstick
Red Velvet
Daisy Chains (Available March 2006)

THE HIDDEN DIARY
Cross My Heart
Make a Wish
Just Between Friends
Take a Bow
Pass It On
Change of Heart

For Granny Vi and
Grandpa Joe,
With Much Love

SANDRA BYRD lives near Seattle with her husband, two children, and a tiny Havanese circus dog named Brie. Besides writing *Island Girl* and the other FRIENDS FOR A SEASON books, Sandra is the bestselling author of the SECRET SISTERS SERIES, THE HIDDEN DIARY SERIES, and the nonfiction book collection GIRLS LIKE YOU.

Learn more about Sandra and her books at *www.friendsforaseason.com*.

CHAPTER ONE

I dragged my suitcase from my room, scraping a thin black line along the wood floor. I turned back, looking one last time. I'd never left home for over a whole month before. There was a naked space on my dresser where my hermit crab bowl normally sat. One of Velveeta's toys peeked from under my bed. I grabbed it and stuffed it into my suitcase. If I couldn't bring my cat, I'd at least take her squeaky.

Dad stepped into my room. "Don't worry,

Quinn. Velveeta will be fine with the Maxwells," he said. "I won't be home enough to keep her happy."

"I know." Really, though, I thought she'd be lost without us. Who would take care of her the way I did? I breathed in the cold winter light pouring through my window. Then I shut the door.

I left my suitcase in the hall and went to check the bathroom. "Tucker! Toothbrush! You're not going for over a month without brushing your teeth."

"Yes, 'Mom,'" he called back in his singsong-sassy voice. It was his way of telling me I had no right to tell him what to do, and it drove me crazy. I, obviously, was not Mom. As if! But someone had to keep tabs on him now since Mom couldn't, not really.

"Fine, let them rot," I said under my breath. He struggled out into the hall with his suitcase, his over-long bangs falling into his eyes. It was a heavy burden for a little kid.

"I'll help," I said more softly this time. He nodded. Tucked under his left arm were his precious note-books.

"Schoolwork?"

"No. Dad already packed that. These are my clip-pings." His hands were too full, and things began to fall. Obsidian, his stuffed dog, slipped. Its fur was well-rubbed with years of loving. Tucker chose to let go of the dog and kept his sweaty fingers gripped on the notebooks. All of his research for Mom was in them. As much as a ten-year-old with a speedy computer could figure out, anyway. I grabbed the dog for him and tucked it under my arm as we walked down the stairs.

"Is there any way we can make this a happy time?" Tucker asked as he took the stairs one by one.

"We will," I promised.

"Ready?" Dad asked.

"Yes." We stepped outside, and Dad turned and locked the door behind us. Mom was already in the front yard, looking as pale as the milky winter sky. All her hair had grown back, though. It looked good.

Dad shook hands with the man who had been in charge of decorating—and now undecorating—our house. Our church was big and we didn't know these people, but they'd come anyway and put the lights up on our house just before Christmas. Now it was Sunday, New Year's Day, a fresh beginning. They were taking the lights down, plucking and popping them off the house like frozen grapes. Dad smiled, always keeping it together in public. But he also cleared his throat, like three times. I knew what that meant.

I walked up behind my mother and put my arms around her waist. She hugged me but then kind of shooed me away. She was saying good-bye to her good friend Dana. I headed toward the car, but I overheard Dana as I did.

"You don't have to do this," Dana said. "It's okay to say no."

It took all of my willpower to keep walking, to pretend I hadn't heard. *No, Doubting Dana, it is not okay to say "no." It isn't your mother. It isn't your choice. So please keep your opinions to yourself unless they're going to help.*

I could literally see steam rising from my face and head into the bitter air. I kept moving.

"I have to try," I heard Mom answer. "I want both time and quality. This is the only way to get it." She coughed. "Maybe."

It was going to work. I knew it was. I just had to believe and remain positive. That's what faith is. Dad closed the trunk and Tucker got into the car. I didn't even care that he was sitting on my side. I don't think he intentionally poached it. I think we were just stressed out enough that nothing seemed normal.

Out of the corner of my eye, I saw a tiny new leaf struggling out of the ground in my mom's flower bed. I bent down and scooped the snow away from it, allowing the sun to pour hope onto this one plant. I willed the tiny crocus to live, to bring early spring and everything warm with it before we got home again.

Mom got into the car and we backed down the

driveway, studded tires biting into the ice before we made it to the bare main roads. I watched my little town of Leavenworth, Washington, roll by—the small, tidy streets where neighbors brought in one another's garbage cans, the tall pine trees standing guard, tips dipped in white chocolate snow.

"Bye," I whispered under my breath. I saw a sign advertising Ribbons in the Snow, the cross-country skiing fund-raiser. I wasn't sure if Mom saw it. I wasn't sure if I should point it out to her or not. I decided not.

"I didn't turn the heat down," Mom said. "Should we go back?"

Dad shook his head. "I'll call Alex and ask him to run over and do it. It'll be okay, Mary." He patted my mother's hand.

"Three hours to drive. That's a lot of time to play I Spy," Mom said to us kids.

I groaned silently. Tucker looked at me. Even *he* was too old for I Spy. We used to play that on car trips when we were little. Neither of us wanted to hurt Mom's feelings, though.

"Sure, Mom." He forced cheerfulness.

Mom laughed, the sweetest sound I know. "I'm just kidding," she said. "How about just one quiz-me question?"

"Okay," I agreed. At home we sometimes take turns

asking a question and then everyone has to answer. Kind of like a family-friendly version of Truth or Dare.

"What's the best thing about New Year's?" Mom asked.

"No yard work for three months," Dad said. Mom elbowed him. "Okay. I guess fresh beginnings. A chance to start something new."

"We're not getting into that healthy eating topic again, are we?" I popped a piece of candy into my mouth from my car stash, then threw the wrapper into the Pit of Death, the cupholder next to my armrest. A mushy apple core was already germinating there, propped in place by hardened chewed gum.

"No, Quinn," Dad said with a vein of humor. "I'm talking about my sagging muscles." He flexed.

"Garden catalogs," Mom said. "Time to start planning." She ruffled a stack of plant catalogs in our direction. My soul filled with sunshine. See? She was planning for spring, summer, and fall!

"This is what I mean about yard work," Dad teased.

"New computer releases," Tucker said.

Dusk fell as we pulled onto the highway that ribboned its way from my hometown through the mountains to Seattle.

"That's what you say for every season," I said.

"So what's your answer, then, smarty?"

"Easy. Valentine's candy in the stores. Nice and

early." I held open the brown bag and showed him my stash.

"Sucrose overdose," Tucker said, turning away.

Mom giggled. She and Dad began to chat about a new car Dad had seen at a dealer's last week. I unzipped the pocket of my backpack. First I checked my wallet—full of Christmas money. Then I drew out a few emails I had printed out because I hadn't had time to read them that morning before we left home. All of my friends would be going back to school tomorrow. So would I—whatever my class would look like. I settled into reading an email from Adam.

Tucker leaned into me. "What was Dana telling Mom?" he whispered.

I leaned back and whispered, "That she doesn't have to have this treatment if she doesn't want it."

Tucker snorted, sharing my disgust. "She needs to mind her own beeswax."

I nodded. For once, we agreed. "It's going to work," I said.

"Of course it is." Tucker looked at me. "Ding-Dong Dana doesn't know anything." He looked at my candy bag. "Gimme some sucrose."

I tossed a chocolate-covered cream heart dressed in red foil. He caught it and then unwrapped it. All of us in the car had hearts like that right now. Soft and squishy on the inside with an extra-thin skin holding it all together.

See? Candy is educational.

Nearly three hours later I elbowed the snoring Tucker, whose mouth was hanging open. "Wake up; we're here. Seattle."

Dad pulled in front of the Anderson House, our home for the next six weeks. "I can park here long enough to unload; then I think I have to bring it around to the lot."

"We ain't in Kansas anymore," I said, looking at the scruffy guys under the streetlamp gripping cigarettes between thumb and pointer fingers. Seattle was big. Leavenworth was small. Leavenworth was home. Seattle was not.

Dad went around and helped Mom out of the car. She shooed him away. "I'm not an invalid, you know." She grabbed her own suitcase, her purse, and her hat, which she'd tucked at her feet.

"Why the hat, Mom?" Tucker asked, nervousness leaking into his voice.

"The cold," Mom said. She tucked a strand of his hair behind his ear. "I'm not going to lose my hair this time."

He smiled and we buzzed the door; the doorman let us in. I'd never lived anywhere with a doorman. Under different circumstances I would have thought this was cool. Like New York City or something. The building was three stories tall, made out of brick. There were twenty-four apartments, eight per floor. It was nice. Like a city apartment.

The man at the desk gave us our keys. "You have a message here from a Miss . . . Kitty?"

Grandma Kitty had already called. Ugh.

"Thank you," Mom said. The man told us where our apartment was—on the second floor—and we headed toward the elevator. I quickly looked around the first floor.

Pop machine. *Cool.*

Rec room. *Cool.*

Laundry room. *Okay.*

We walked to the elevator and pushed the button. It opened, and before we could step in a girl and an older man stepped out. Her hair was blond and wavy, but her skin was kind of pasty, like she hadn't had any exercise for a while. The older man—he looked like her dad, wavy blond hair, too—had circles under his eyes.

"Hi," Dad said to them. The man nodded politely but didn't answer. The girl and I locked eyes. Then she stepped out to the first floor, and we stepped into the elevator.

I don't know why it unnerved me, but it did. Maybe because she and I looked to be the same age

and no one was at Anderson House for a fun vacation—or really, even because they wanted to be. Everyone here was in trouble.

Dad led us to our apartment and unlocked the
door. "Two bedrooms," I said. I hadn't thought about
that. I'd be sharing a room with Tucker.

"All right." I yanked him into the room and shut
the door. "Ground rules. I don't look in your notebooks, you don't read my stuff. No emails, no journals,
nothing. If I catch you going through my stuff, you're
dead and I don't care what anyone says."

"I don't care about your sappy letters from Adam
or screeching emails from that pack of cats you call
friends," he said. "Just keep out of my notebooks so
they don't get chocolate smudges on them or anything
gets out of place."

We understood each other perfectly. I put my stuff
away, making sure the pictures of my friends were on
the shelf by my bed. Holly and I goofing off at Crazy
Hair Day. Adam and his buddies on their skis. I put the
invitation to the Valentine's party up there, too, just to
remind me I had something to look forward to. In the
living room Dad set up the computer we'd brought
from home. Mom called Grandma Kitty.

I walked out into the living room. "Going back
home tomorrow?" I asked Dad.

"If the roads are okay and Grandma Kitty gets here

on time," Dad said. "I'll be back next weekend, though, and every weekend." Dad didn't have much vacation time left, and no sick time, even though his boss had been good during the years of sickness.

We had hamburgers from a nearby drive-through for dinner. A last supper, you might say, before Grandma Kitty arrived. I had some extra fries.

In the middle of the night I woke up. For a minute I forgot where I was. My hair was sweaty, but the room wasn't too warm. Tucker snored in the bed next to mine. Somehow, the noise was soothing.

I thought I heard my dad crying softly in the living room. I wasn't sure. Maybe dads only cry in the middle of the night. It scared me. I watched the minutes flash by on the red digital clock.

In the morning Tucker and I got ready for school. Fitzschool was for kids who were here getting treatment—or whose parents were getting treatment. This way they didn't fall totally behind in their own schools when they went back home.

"How big is the school?" Tucker asked. I watched

the clock for his whole two minutes of tooth-brushing.

"I think there's like fifteen kids in each class. You'll be in the lower class, with all the kids sixth grade and under." He looked crushed.

"Where will you be?" He swished with water.

"Upstairs, with the high schoolers."

He spit into the sink. "You are *not* in high school."

"I am, I will remind you, a *pre-freshman*." I flipped my head upside down and brushed. I'd read that was how you build volume into hair. "Besides, high school here is seventh through twelfth grade."

We both kissed Mom and Dad good-bye. Dad would head home to Leavenworth before we got back from school.

"I'll be up the hill starting treatment later," Mom reminded us, pointing to the hospital. "Grandma Kitty will be here."

"Okay. Can I come up to see you?" I asked.

Mom nodded. "Quinn can. But Tucker, you have to be over twelve in order to get into these treatment rooms. I'm sorry, buddy. I'll be home on Wednesday."

He nodded. "Don't let them give you any vitamins. Or orange juice or grapefruit juice. I read that it can interfere with treatment."

"I won't." Mom kissed his cheek. "See what new information you can find out in two days."

Tucker brightened. "I will."

Tucker and I walked through the long hallway that connected Anderson House to Fitzschool, the school attached to the Fitzsimmons Cancer Care Center. When we got back to our apartment, Mom would be gone.

"Exactly who goes to school here?" Tucker asked, twisting his finger back and forth through his belt loop.

"Kids who are sick, sometimes, but mostly kids like you and me whose parents are here having cancer treatment. Kids who live far away."

"We don't live that far away," Tucker said.

"I know, but Mom wanted us here," I reminded him. It was odd. In the past, she'd always wanted things to remain *normal*. Whatever that was. I shut the hallway door behind us.

We walked into the school lobby and the receptionist met us. "Hi. I'll show you to your classes." I admired her cool streaked hair and awesome shoes.

Tucker's class was downstairs. There were lots of tables in his classroom, but no desks. The walls were painted in bright, happy colors. As if.

My room was upstairs, next to the library. I walked into the room and all the voices went silent. The walls were papered with maps, and there were rows of shelves to the side where different texts stood stacked. Hooks laden with backpacks lined one wall. I looked around the tables. All of the seats were taken.

"Hey." The girl I'd seen in the elevator yesterday stood up. "You can sit here. I'll get another chair."

"Thank you," I said. She pulled up a chair right next to me and everyone went back to work. I needed a friend here. I smiled at her.

She lowered her head to her work.

The teacher got me settled in and then went back to the student she had been working with. She seemed okay, too. I wasn't planning to get to know her real well. I'd be out of here soon.

The vibe in the room was different. Everyone was a citizen of Planet Cancer. I was so used to people looking at me. *That's the girl whose mom has cancer*, I read in their pitying eyes. No one looked at me like that here. I breathed out. It was reassuring in some strange way.

We worked on science for a while, and then everyone did their own math, whatever their school at home was doing. Fitzschool had called my school in Leavenworth and gotten my math work. I couldn't afford to get behind. At twelve-thirty a bell rang. I kind of stood there while everyone else scattered and chattered.

"If you want a friend you have to be a friend" came back to my mind. Grandma Kitty again. There was no escaping her, even in the privacy of my own head.

I walked up to the yellow-haired girl. "What do we do now?"

"Eat lunch," she said. "Since we can't bring friends to our apartments, we all eat here most of the time. Did you bring your lunch?"

I shook my head. *Tucker!* He had no lunch either.

"There are always a couple of spares in the fridge down in the lunchroom," she said. "In case anyone forgets. Come with me, I'll show you."

I followed her downstairs. She seemed so tired. Maybe she was a cancer patient herself.

She opened the fridge and took out a brown bag.

"Do you think it'd be okay to take one for my brother?" I asked.

"Sure." She took another one out and handed it to me.

"Thanks," I said. I walked over to Tucker and handed him his lunch. He nodded but was engrossed in talking computer stuff with two other kids his age. I looked around. There were a couple of girls who looked to be older high schoolers on a bench in the corner of the room. I could sit with them. I heard them giggle, and they looked friendly. And fun. One waved to me. I needed some fun!

The yellow-haired girl sat on a window seat, slowly eating her lunch. *I'll bet she could use some fun, too,* came an unbidden thought. I sighed. *Yes, Lord.*

"Is anyone sitting here?" I asked, moving toward the window seat.

She shook her head and scooted over.

"I'm Quinn Miller," I said. "I moved in yesterday."

"I'm Annie Meyer." She took a bite of her apple. "I saw you. Where are you from?"

"Leavenworth."

"Kansas?" Her eyes sparked for the first time. I hated to douse them again.

"No, Washington. It's about three hours east over the mountains."

"Oh. I'm from Olathe, Kansas," she said.

I started to giggle. She looked at me.

"It's just that when we drove up yesterday, I said to myself, 'Quinn, you're not in Kansas anymore.' You know, from *The Wizard of Oz*? It's even funnier to think when you pulled up you really *weren't* in Kansas anymore."

Annie smiled again, which made her look really pretty. "I've been here for six weeks. My mom has six more weeks of chemo."

So she *wasn't* sick. Her mom was. I didn't know what the protocol was here. I mean, do I ask her how her mom is doing, do we pretend cancer doesn't exist, does she ask me? I hadn't met anyone my own age whose mom had cancer. Besides me.

"What are you here for?" she asked.

"My mom has stage four breast cancer."

"Stage four?"

"End stage, kind of," I said. The sun warmed my shoulders and made Annie's hair light as an angel's. It was deceiving, though. I knew how cold it was outside.

"Is she . . ." she started to ask and then stopped and blushed.

I just couldn't say the word *dying*. "It's in her lungs, but this new treatment, if it works, should be able to give her a few more years before it gets into her brain and liver. Then we can have a good, long time with her." It sounded so factual coming out. I know, because I'd had to tell all of my friends at school and church the exact same words. Inside, though, it felt like ripping off a scab over and over again.

"Your mom looked so good," Annie said. "When I saw her yesterday. Better than my mom."

"Stage four people usually look healthier than people whose cancer isn't so bad," I said. "Because there is no use in giving them harsh treatments anymore." I wanted to change the topic. "How about your mom?"

"We're on the second round of chemo. She's going to get better, though. The doctor said he'd never seen such an easy patient. It'll probably be like it never happened. That's why we're here. This is the best place to get totally cured."

My chest hurt for Annie. Black-haired, green-eyed me looked into the face of blond, blue-eyed Annie and saw an exact reflection of myself three years ago, when my mom was at stage two and they thought it would be gone for good.

"I hope your mom's treatment works," Annie said.

"It will." I bit into the PB and J. No sweets in the bag, I noticed. Ah well. I had plenty at home. That is, if Grandma Kitty hadn't "picked up."

I stood. "I guess I'd better get my brother and get home. I'm going to visit my mom this afternoon. She's starting a new treatment." Fitzschool only went from nine until twelve-thirty. The afternoons were for field trips. Or family.

"My mom, too," Quinn said. "Her chemo always starts on Monday. That way she feels better on the weekends."

"Do you want to walk up to the hospital together?" I asked.

Annie gazed at me with a look of wonder. "I *never* go for her treatments. The rooms stink, my mom says. And it's easier on her when we're not there. She said that the first day. We don't ever talk about treatment or cancer things."

I almost dropped my empty lunch bag. They didn't ever talk about it?

"Oh well, maybe you can come over sometime," I said instead.

"We're not allowed in each other's apartments," Annie said. "Contamination if someone has a cold, or something."

I nodded. *Have it your way.* "Okay. See ya."

She nodded back. "Bye."

Tucker and I walked back to the apartment, Tucker chattering the whole way about his new friends. But all I could think about was my old ones.

I stuck my key into the hole, but before I could unlock the door Grandma Kitty opened it from the inside.

I could smell them from the hallway—fresh vegetables. She'd brought the Vegematic.

"Hello, dears." She bustled us into the apartment. "Come on in and have a snack. I brought some flaxseed cookies. Quinn, did you go to school without a jacket?"

"I didn't even leave the building, Grandma," I said.

"Always be prepared," she said, returning to the kitchen. "What if there'd been an earthquake?"

I looked at Tucker, who fled the room before he busted up.

"Your mom called and said they'd be starting late so you didn't have to go up. I figured you'd probably have homework and said I'd suggest you stay home.

That you'd see her on Wednesday."

"Did she say I had to stay home?" I asked.

"No, no, it just seemed best."

"Well, I want to go," I said. At home, Dad or Dana always stayed with Mom for the first day of treatment. I didn't want her to be alone.

Grandma Kitty pursed her lips but said nothing.

Round One—Quinn.

I walked up the hill to the hospital, hopped on the elevator with lots of other Planet Cancer people in stocking caps, and arrived on the fifth floor. I walked down the hallway, stopping at each door to look for my mom's chart. I stood outside Room 512. This was it. The hallway was long and light. I think the reason they use those fluorescent lights in hospitals is because that is often the only source of brightness. Fake light. I got ready to push open the proper door—and then stopped.

I heard a voice.

"What kind of shadow?"

"It's probably nothing to worry about," a woman's voice said. "We'll check it again when the treatment is over. In the meantime, let me know if you notice any-thing different—physically, mentally, whatever."

My shoulder bumped against the propped door and it squeaked. My cover was blown. I pushed the door open and tried to pretend like I hadn't been listening. I was really embarrassed to eavesdrop on my mom. I hadn't meant to, though.

"Quinn!" my mom said, her voice filled with pleasure. The vinyl recliner swallowed her up; the meds pump stood behind her, holding two bags that dripped through snaky clear tubes and into my mom's chest through the tube that had been inserted there permanently. The room, as always, smelled of bleach and stainless steel. "This is my daughter," Mom said to the doctor.

"Is Quinn a family name?" the doctor asked. "It's so unusual."

Mom laughed. "No. My name, Mary, is so plain that I wanted something unusual for my daughter. I'd thought about having a daughter for a long time and wanted something fun."

The doctor smiled and snapped her file shut. "You picked a wonderful name. Let the nurse know if you need anything. I'll check on you before I leave tonight."

Mom nodded and her doctor left. I sat down on the chair beside Mom's recliner. "Did you just start?"

"Yeah. They had to run some tests first," she said. She must have seen my alarm because she reached out and touched my hand. "Nothing to fret about."

I nodded.

"How was school?" she asked.

I opened up my backpack and yanked out my

notebook and told her what we were studying in each class. "Earth science, just like at home. Algebra II, of course. I'm already way ahead. Writing conventionals. Blech." Mom liked me to tell her the details, I know. It kept her involved in my education.

"What's that?" Mom pointed to a list on the last page.

"Um, my New Year's resolutions." I pulled the journal close.

"I won't look. You'll achieve them all, I bet. Do them sooner rather than later. You never know what the year will hold." Mom closed her eyes and rested her head on the back of the easy chair.

"You might not say sooner is better than later if you knew what was on here," I teased. She smiled softly, eyes still closed.

You never know what the year will hold.

You just never know.

Mom fell asleep. I left two conversation heart candies on the table beside her chair. *You Rock!* said one, and *Call Me*, the other. Then I left the rest of the large box in case she wanted something sweet later on.

Quinn's New Year's Resolutions

#1 Help mom stay healthy.
#2 Drive a car before any of my friends. I
     am not kidding. Otherwise I will ONCE
     AGAIN be last since all my friends will
     turn 15 before I do. I just want to be
     first, at one thing that is important, for
     once.
#3 Make an unhealthy meal that Grandma
     Kitty says tastes delicious.
#4 Get kissed by a boy. Not Tucker.

CHAPTER TWO

I can leave some barley soup. It will be no trouble at all to make some before I go. A big pot. With fish oil. Fish oil is a great source of omega–3 fatty acids." Grandma Kitty—also known and loved by us as G Kitty— untied her apron and hung it on the copper cup hook she'd placed by the small stove.

"No, Ma, it's okay. Tom is taking us out to dinner tonight," Mom answered. It was so good to have my mom here with us in the apartment.

She'd stayed in the hospital till Wednesday and slept a lot on Thursday, but today she was feeling really good. Dad had promised to take us out in Seattle tonight. School was over. It was a real weekend. Who knew what lay ahead? Life had thus far taught me that there are surprises—good and bad—around every corner.

Tucker sighed, relieved not to have to stomach the soup. Then his head snapped up. "Where *is* Dad, anyway?" He checked his watch. "He's late."

Mom covered his hand with hers. "It's okay, buddy," she said. "Nothing bad is going to happen to Dad."

Tucker's face softened. Mom knew what he'd been thinking.

Grandma Kitty kissed Mom on both cheeks and then zipped her boots on. "You sure Tom won't mind picking me up on Sunday afternoon?" For the whole time we were in Seattle, G Kitty would be staying with us from Sunday night to Friday afternoon and then go home for the weekend. To rest, I know. And leave us some family time.

"I'm sure it'll be okay, Ma. Tell Dad to have a good time at the car show, and he can come get you next Friday. We'll all visit with him then."

"Okay. Tucker, I hemmed your pants." Grandma Kitty slipped her hand into the sleeve of a raincoat and tied a plastic rain hat over her silver hair. "I don't want you running around that school looking like a lost little boy. And, Quinn, I'll sew up the hole in the knee of your jeans when I get back."

I opened my mouth to say I *liked* that small hole in the knee of my jeans and that Tucker *liked* his pants long. But I caught Mom's eye. So I said nothing at all.

Grandma Kitty kissed my cheek, too. The skin under her eyes slumped tiredly toward her cheeks. I kissed her back. After all, it had been a long week for all of us.

After she'd closed the door, we sat there, waiting for Dad. Tucker watched TV and scanned the periodic table of elements, marking those of interest—of interest!—with yellow sticky flags. I emailed Adam, trying to shield the screen so my mom couldn't read it. Not that she would. On purpose, anyway.

"I invited a new friend to come to dinner with us tonight," Mom said. "I met her on the fifth floor this week."

Trust Mom to make a new friend. "Who is that?"

"Her name is Mercy. Her treatment room is near mine. She's here getting chemo. Her daughter is about your age, which is what brought us into our first conversation."

"Let me guess," I said, "her daughter's name is Annie."

"Right!" Mom said. "Have you met her?"

"Yes." I clicked the key on the computer keyboard

to send the email, wrote a fast one to the Pack of Cats, as Tucker called them, and turned to face Mom. No sense telling her that I'd already tried to be friends with Annie but she hadn't been really excited about it. She answered if I talked with her but hadn't sought me out on her own. I'd been eating lunch with the fun and funny high schoolers. Besides, I had friends at home. Friends I'd see soon.

"I thought chemo patients weren't supposed to go out. Or have visitors. You know, cross-contamination."

"Don't you remember? We went out from time to time when I was getting chemo the first time. Not a lot—but enough to keep me sane."

"When I talked with Annie, I got the feeling they didn't go out much." I turned the computer monitor off and then faced my mom again.

"They haven't. I encouraged her to come, though, and said we'd leave if they sat us by a coughing kid." Mom's eyes twinkled. "I know we want some family time, but I felt like she needs a break and wouldn't go without an invitation. She's been in her apartment for five weeks. Through Christmas, even."

"Oh." That might explain Annie's pale face. Surely *she* got out, though.

"What's new on email?" Mom nodded toward the now-quiet computer. By now she was checking her watch.

"Nothing. Everyone just making sure we'll be home in time for the Valentine's party at church."

"What did you tell them?"

"I said *of course* we will." I looked up nervously. "We will, won't we?"

"Of course." Mom grinned. She'd been teasing me. We'd all been looking forward to going. There'd be a live band, catered food, and five hundred people. Four hundred ninety-nine people—and Adam.

Just then Dad walked in. All of us burst toward him. "Dad!" I threw my arms around him and Tucker hugged his waist.

I saw where Dad was looking. At Mom.

"How do you feel?"

"Great," she said. "Ready to go?"

"Ready," he said.

Mom called Annie's mom and they met us in the lobby. Since it was Friday, Annie's mom was feeling good, too, though Annie's dad seemed a bit nervous to be leaving Anderson House. We caravaned together to Johnny Rockets and ate up.

"Can I play the jukebox?" Tucker asked. He fed quarter after quarter through the lips of the coin holder as he tried to decide what tunes to play.

"Can I pick one?" Mom asked.

"Yeah." Tucker swung the small table selector toward Mom.

Mom chose one, the song came on, and Dad groaned. "Not that seventies disco stuff again."

Mom grinned—Dad hated disco. She liked being a pest. I take after my mom.

Annie didn't say much the whole meal, but she did sit next to me. On purpose. She could have sat in one of several other seats at the long table.

"What can I get for you?" asked the young Asian waitress who came to take our order.

Annie looked at her mom. Her dad looked at the table. All of a sudden there was a weird, tense vibe. Even my parents felt it, I know, because my dad cleared his throat. He only does that when he's uncomfortable. No one said anything, though. I tried to figure out what was wrong. Maybe they were worried the waitress was sick. She wasn't sniffling or anything, though.

Soon she brought our food, plates resting from her wrist all the way up her left arm as she dealt them to us like cards, one after the other. Annie picked at the red leather seat and then she picked at her burger.

We chatted and she told me some about her friends back home, and I told her about mine. Even about Adam. She didn't have a crush in Kansas, she said, but then she stopped talking. Aha! There was something behind that. We might have been friends even if we weren't both on Planet Cancer.

Every time the waitress came back, though, things got weird. Finally we finished eating and got up to go back to Anderson House. My mom hugged Mercy, Annie's mom.

I asked Annie, "Do you want to go to Starbucks tomorrow morning?" I knew my parents were planning to work on a school project with Tucker in the morning. I thought I'd give them some space.

All right, so I had an ulterior motive. I wanted to see if Annie would tell me what the scoop was with the waitress.

Annie said, "Yeah, sure." We agreed to meet in the lobby at nine-thirty the next morning.

That night, after my mom was asleep and Tucker was asleep, a noise in the living room woke me up. I looked at the clock. It was three o'clock in the morning. I peeked out the door. My dad was playing a World War II computer game. He was the shooter. My dad had never played computer games before my mom got sick. I tiptoed back to bed and felt that fear crawl over me again. It made my skin prickle.

As soon as I woke up the next morning, I looked out the window. "Rain, rain, go away. Come again another day." I yanked the curtains closed so I could get dressed. How did people live here when it rained all day every day? But I had one good thing to look forward to: coffee with Annie. So far no one had told me I had to drink decaffeinated coffee drinks. I was hoping to make it out of the apartment without a word.

I could hear Tucker in the living room, so I locked the door and got dressed. Before I left the room to brush my teeth, I looked at myself sideways in the mirror. Shouldn't I be filling out a little bit more? I mean, some of my friends looked a lot more, um, womanly than I did. If you know what I mean.

I wondered if my mom felt womanly still. Since the mastectomy, I mean.

I turned my head upside down and brushed, then yanked my hair back into a ponytail and pulled it partway through so there was a little bun and a little splay of hair. At least my hair was full.

Annie's face lit up as I met her in the lobby. "Ready?" she asked. I nodded and we headed out the door to walk the block or so to Starbucks. She didn't look pale today. She looked positively styling. I felt like a fashion flunky beside her.

"Do you drink a lot of coffee at home?" I asked.

She shook her head. "Never. I think we have a Starbucks in Olathe now, but I haven't been there."

"I don't drink a lot of coffee at home, either. My mom hasn't been too hip on it. Coffee added to my sugar habit isn't a good mix, she said."

"Sugar habit?" Annie said.

"You'll see," I said as we stepped inside the coffee shop, "if you get to know me."

Surprisingly, the two comfy chairs by the fireplace were open. "How about you sit here and guard these and I'll go get our drinks," I said.

"Okay."

"What do you want?"

Annie looked at a loss. "I don't know. What do you usually get?"

"I'll just get us something good," I promised and went to the counter. I'd hardly had *any* of the drinks on the menu board. I had received a Starbucks card in my stocking this year in spite of my parents' coffee worries. I knew they were cutting me a break while we were here in Seattle.

There were a lot of people in line. I took my wallet out of my purse to get my Starbucks card and grabbed my notebook, too. While I waited I wrote down the names of some drinks I *had* to have before my card ran out of credit.

"What can I get started for you?" the barista finally asked.

"Two tall peppermint mochas," I said. She nodded and got to work.

When I got back to the soft chairs, Annie moved her purse. She'd put it on the other chair to save a space for me. "How much do I owe you?"

"You can pay next time," I said. "That way I'll know there'll be a next time, for sure."

She smiled at me and sat there sipping. "Yum! Awesome choice!"

I had to agree—it was like a smooth, hot peppermint patty skating on my tongue. Annie set her cup down on the small triangular table between us. She took a piece of cloth and a needle out of her bag and worked while we talked.

It was kind of strange. None of my friends did stuff like that. "What are you making?"

"Head wraps," she said.

Yeah, I had noticed one on her mom last night. Kind of like a scarf, but not so much material. It was very cool.

"Can I see?"

She handed it over to me and I turned it right side out. It was bright blue with sparkles throughout it. It would look pretty and bright and match her mom's eyes. "This is so cool. I have never seen anything like it."

She nodded. "Me neither. But my mom didn't like the scarves that made her look like a fifties movie star. And I sew. And I'm bored in the apartment when I'm not at school or out with my dad, so it seemed like a good thing to do. If I had my machine here I could whip up quite a few."

I sipped my mocha. Totally, totally awesome. Sugar, heat, chocolate, smoothness. I could feel the caffeine zipping through my veins. Okay, maybe not yet. But it'd come. "So, do you sew a lot?"

"I made these." She pointed to her outfit. Her jean skirt was awesome because it was cut unlike any other I had ever seen—narrow without being tight. Her top was a new design to me, too—a peach overshirt connected to a shirt underneath without being bulky or showing too much. "I want to study fashion' design when I graduate," Annie said.

"You know, I just had a great idea." I set my cup down. "You could make up a whole bunch of those head wraps and sell them. I'm serious. There are tons of people that would wear them right here. Look around! You could make a fortune! Yours are so much cuter than anything I've seen. My mom would have loved those when she lost her hair." Now that my mom was stage four, the treatments were softer, prolonging life rather than killing cells, so she kept her hair.

There were a few women with scarves on their heads right there in the coffee shop, and beyond the window was the cancer center.

"I don't know anyone at home who has cancer. We're leaving soon and my mom's hair will grow back, and I'm not good at sales or organizing things anyway."

She must have realized how harsh it sounded. She added, "Thanks anyway."

I settled back into my chair. Okaaaayyy . . . next topic. "So, are you excited to go back home, then? I am. We're going to be back in time for a huge Valentine's party at my church."

"Oh, how fun!" Annie lit up. "Tell me about it."

So I did. "Our youth group is helping organize it. My friend Holly did the invitations—she's the one that gets everyone going. I have another friend who is totally into fashion—like you! She's doing table decorations. I'm the organizer, but, um, I'm not really able to do that much anymore. I mean, since I'm here. I'm going to do the flowers, though. And Adam is going to make sure we get tickets," I said. "Since we won't be there to buy them ahead of time."

"Adam?" Annie asked.

"You know, the guy I mentioned last night."

"Your crush?" Annie asked.

"Yeah."

"Is it returned?" she asked.

"Yeah," I said, blushing. "It is."

She smiled. "Have you noticed Ben in class?"

"At school here?" *Ben, Ben* . . . I tried to think which one was Ben.

"The tall one," Annie helpfully supplied.

"Ah, yeah. He's cute," I agreed. I mean, it was obvious where this was leading. I didn't want her to think I thought he was *too* cute, but I also didn't want her to think I thought her crush was a dog.

"At home," Annie said, "my friend Beth and I are the tallest of our friends. So whenever there's a tall guy she whispers 'tall guy alert' to me so I know to pay attention."

I giggled. Adam wasn't very tall. But neither was I. Annie didn't have a crush at home. But she did here.

Annie took a sip of her coffee and started sewing again. The fabric was soft and elegant at the same time. "Beth's aunt had breast cancer a few years ago."

"Oh. How did that go?" I asked. The rain was letting up outside. The sun was coming up for air.

"She died. After many surgeries and rounds of treatment." Annie's needle plied the fabric, in and out and up and down in a soothing rhythm.

I guess I felt that since she brought the subject up, I could push it a little. "Is that what you're afraid of?"

She looked up at me. "Aren't you?"

I said nothing. I didn't need to.

"My mom would love your Valentine's party at church," Annie said. "She loves Valentine's Day. It's her favorite holiday."

"Doesn't your church have a party like that?"

Annie shook her head. "We don't have a church. Anyway, we don't leave here until the day after Valentine's Day. Our tickets are all bought and paid for. We're going home and pretending that this never happened!"

Two girls walked in the door, shook the rain off of their coats, and giggled past us. They were probably a few years older than we were. I noticed Annie's eyes follow them. She set her sewing down and got that weird look on her face, the one she had last night with the waitress.

I wanted to ask her what was up. Then I realized— the waitress last night was Asian and so were these girls. There was obviously something going on. But I felt like our friendship was as fragile as our feelings right now. Life was already too hard. I wasn't going to make it harder. She'd tell me, in time. I knew she would.

Annie picked up her head wrap again.

"I don't have any friends who sew," I said.

She didn't look up. "You do now."

We walked home together, and when I got into the apartment my mom was laughing and my dad was laughing and my brother was rolling his eyes.

I am thankful for things I never thought I'd be thankful for. "Okay, I'm the one who had the caffeine. What's going on?"

"Oh, Tucker was just clowning," Mom said. "I'm sending them to the store to buy a few things Grandma

Kitty left on her list." I stood still. "And a few things she didn't." Mom giggled and I laughed with her.

"Can I stay here with you?"

She nodded. "I hope you will." The guys left and she booted up the computer. "Look what came!"

She pulled an email onto the screen. It was from my parents' Sunday school class at home. "They listed every hour of the day, and someone is praying for me round the clock, all day and night, for the whole time we're here. That means someone is up even in the middle of the night praying! Isn't that amazing?"

I wondered if I should email them and have the three o'clock in the morning person pray for Dad. "That's so cool, Mom. The treatment is going to work, I know it! Everything is going to be okay."

"Dana and Debbie are coming on Wednesday to visit for an hour or two. They'll be here in Seattle to do some buying for Debbie's husband's business. So—I have something to look forward to this week."

"Will you be here? You won't still be at the hospital?"

"I'll be here," Mom said. "And not *too* tired. Last week, the first week of treatment, was the hardest." She stood up and headed toward the kitchen. But as she reached the hallway, she stumbled and lost her balance. Just in time she grabbed the back of a chair.

"Are you okay?" I threw my purse to the ground to

"Number one is what I want most," I said. "How can I help you stay healthy?"

"You can pray for me. And you can help with Tucker and with Grandma Kitty. I know you know those things."

"I want to do more," I said. "But I can't."

"You can't," Mom agreed. "It's hard to not have any control, isn't it?"

I nodded and a tear slipped down my cheek. "Don't go, Mom. Don't go." I snuggled up under her arm. She wiped away my tear with her thumb and kissed it, like she used to do when I was a little girl. Then she picked up the list again.

"Drive a *car*?" Mom kept reading. "You're barely fourteen!"

I giggled. "I know, I know. But every one of my friends turns fifteen before I do, so that means they are all going to get their permits before I do. If I do it at fourteen, then for *once* I get to do something first."

Mom giggled with me. "Did I ever tell you about when I first drove?"

I shook my head.

"Grandpa Doug took me into a high school parking lot in his old car. He drove me around twice and said, 'Well, kid, that's about it.' He got out, I got behind the driver's seat, and he took me onto the Wiser Lake Road."

"You're kidding."

"Nope. It's just a country road, you know, up by their house in Lynden. He thought that because he was such a car buff, his only kid would be, too."

"Were you?"

"Of course. Till I crashed into a driveway pole."

"Did he get totally mad?"

Mom shook her head. "Nope. But he's never let me drive his Mustang. Not even now."

I laughed. My grandpa loves cars. When I was a little girl I thought his name was Grandpa Dog since Grandma was Grandma Kitty. I finally figured out his name is Doug. But I still call him Grandpa Dog once in a while just to pester him.

"So can I drive, then?"

"A tractor," Mom said. I didn't know if she was kidding or not. I didn't ask.

Mom rubbed her head a little, like she had a headache, but she kept reading the list. "I will do an Irish jig right here in this room if Grandma Kitty says an unhealthy meal is good," she said. She lowered her voice, even though no one else was in the room. "But I happen to know she loves a good, creamy, very unhealthy fettuccini carbonara. You didn't hear that from me."

I smiled.

Mom moved on. "Kiss a boy? Any particular boy?"

"Let's not talk about that one," I said, snapping the book shut.

"I'm going to call Grandma Kitty," Mom said, a dreamy look in her eyes. "I want her to bring something for you when she comes tomorrow. I think you'll find it fun—and special. And different."

"What is it?" I love surprises.

"You'll see." Mom stood up. I was so relieved to notice that she didn't seem shaky on her feet anymore.

She headed into her room to whisper her phone call. I picked up my notebook and reviewed the list I'd written in Starbucks.

Quinn's List of Drinks I must Have While in Seattle, Before my Starbucks Card Runs Out of Credit

#1 Hazelnut white chocolate mocha with extra whipped cream

#2 Green Tazo tea with two packs of raw sugar

#3 Chantico Drinking Chocolate

#4 Double espresso. Straight up.

CHAPTER THREE

The next morning we went to a small church service at the hospital; it was held in a room called the "Sanctuary." I don't know why they don't call it a chapel. They call it a chapel at the hospital by home. We went because Mom wanted to go. There weren't many people there. I felt connected with them, not just because we all worshiped Jesus but because we were all caught in the same spider's web.

I'm glad to be together again in this way, I said

to God in my head, *in a kind of church*. I felt His warmth grow inside me.

After we got home, Mom drew me aside. "Do you mind going to get Grandma Kitty with Dad? He has to pick her up. I think he could use the company."

"But then I won't get to be with *you*," I said. Being in the hospital—even in the Sanctuary—had made me nervous for my mom.

"You get to come with me when I start the second week of treatment tomorrow," she said, pointing outside—to the hospital, I guess. "Tucker can't. I need some time alone with him, and Dad needs company before he drives back to Leavenworth tonight."

I agreed, reluctantly.

Tucker and Mom, armed with a bowl of popcorn, gathered around the computer to start the game Dad had brought back for them. Mom was already in her slippers and robe.

Dad and I set out to Lynden to get Grandma Kitty. Her friend Mabel had taken her home on Friday, so this was the first time I'd been back at her house in a few months.

It was two hours each way. I'd packed lots of snacks for the road, which we'd have to eat on the way there since G Kitty was sure to sniff at it on the way home.

"Chocolate-covered peanut butter heart?" I held it

toward my dad. He snapped it up. It was nice to have a dad that you could always count on. "So how was work this week?"

"Fine," he said. "I had a hard time concentrating with you guys gone." He licked the chocolate off of his fingers. "I played a lot of games on Tucker's computer at night."

"Did it help you sleep?" I said.

"No," he answered. "But it's something I always win at."

I nodded. "That's why I like math."

Dad looked at me. "What do you mean?"

"If you do the right thing, follow the right procedure, you always get the right answer. If it comes out wrong, you can go back, find the mistake, do it over, and it comes out right." I always got A's in math. It bugged Tucker. That was the only reason I tried so hard. The other was that I loved the simplicity, the pattern, the art of it. I was in control. I had no control over almost anything else in life right now.

The road went on and on and the rain continued to fall and fall, crying down the windshield no matter how quickly the blades wiped it away.

I nibbled Nerds and read *The Return of the King*. As we drew near town, I giggled when we passed Wiser Lake Road. I could just see my mom in Grandpa Doug's old car, creeping down that road.

Finally we pulled up at their house. The yard, like the house, was spotless. I tumbled out of the car and into the kitchen.

"Take your shoes off!" Grandma Kitty hollered at me as I ran toward the bathroom. I kicked them to the side, and after I was done I mopped up the small puddle of muddy water they'd left behind.

"All ready, Mom?" Dad asked her. I thought it was kind of neat that he called her that. His own parents had died when he was young.

"Almost, dear," Grandma Kitty said. She always called him "dear." Mom teased that G Kitty liked Dad better than she liked her. "I have a few things to get out of the pantry." She took a big basket in there with her and began loading up. Visions of Little Red Riding Hood and *her* basket and *her* grandma crossed my mind. I willed them away out of respect. With a smile.

"Oh, Quinn, I'm so glad you came, too," G Kitty called from the pantry. "Your mother asked for a box from the attic, and I just can't get up there anymore. The arthritis is much worse when it rains like this, and I can't climb the stairs. Would you go and get it for me?"

The surprise!

"Sure, Grandma," I said. "What does the box look like?"

"It says 'Diaries' on the outside of it. I think it's

toward the back. Behind the Ping-Pong table."

Diaries! Sweet!

I went upstairs and peeked into the bedroom that had been Mom's when she was a girl. It still had the same fuzzy purple chenille bedspread with a stuffed poodle dog on the pillow. I couldn't resist—I snuck in and ran my hand over the curds of fabric, letting it tickle the palm of my hand. I liked to sleep here whenever I spent the night.

Back out on the landing, I reached for the cord that hung from the ceiling and pulled down the collapsible stairway to the attic so that I could climb up. The attic was dusty, of course. Especially since Grandma couldn't get up there anymore. I pulled the string on the one lone bulb that hung in the middle and let my eyes adjust. Two sneezes later I was ready to find the box.

The Ping-Pong table stood unsteadily on thin, wobbly legs. I was careful not to bump it as I stepped behind.

I found the box. "Diaries" was marked on the outside in neat permanent marker. It was Mom's handwriting.

I flipped open the top flap. There were five or six journals inside. Each one had a piece of masking tape across the front with a year written on it. I figured the dates out in my head. It looked like seventh grade through graduation.

I took out the eighth-grade diary and ran my finger over the top. A little bit of dust came off but not much. My mom had held this in *her* hands when she was my age. What were her hopes? Her dreams? Did she have secrets? I knew, as annoying as Grandma Kitty could be, she wouldn't read Mom's diaries. She was irritating and bossy, but she wasn't a snoop.

Neither was I. The pull to open that diary and read it was as strong as the moon on the tide, but I overcame temptation and put it back into the box with the others. I dragged the box away from the wall and got ready to carry it down.

Then I saw her.

She huddled behind the box, overlooked—or hidden, it seemed—slipped into a small nook between the diary box and a box of forgotten Christmas ornaments.

I picked her up and brushed her off. There was a small crack across her forehead—wrinkled a little, like Mom's—but her lips were still painted pouty pink. Her hair was wavy and blond. Kind of like Annie's! Most beautiful of all—even for a girl like me who was never into dolls—was her gorgeous red velvet dress.

She had to have belonged to my mother. Whose else would she be?

I grabbed the box in one arm and the doll in the

other and pulled on the light string with my teeth. "*Good* night", it seemed to say in a two-syllable blink off. I climbed backward down the attic stairs.

Grandma's pantry basket was done. Stuffed with kale and Chinese herbs, I'm sure. "If there was anything else I thought would help Mary . . ." Grandma Kitty muttered as she rooted around the shelves. "What could there be?"

Dad looked like he was ready to go. It was two hours back to Seattle, then three more back to Leavenworth for him.

"Did you get some coffee, Dad?" I asked, setting the box and doll on the table. He nodded and held up his travel mug.

G Kitty's eyes opened wide, and she looked so surprised I thought her hair was going to peel off.

"*Where* did you find *that*?" She pointed an accusing finger at the doll.

"Behind the box. Was it my mom's?"

"Yes," she said, clapping her hands one against the other as if cleaning herself of garden dirt. "But I don't think she'll be too pleased to see it. Best not take it."

Grandma Kitty was used to people agreeing with her pronouncements. She turned and walked out the door to tuck her suitcase full of fresh aprons and day slacks into the car without a look back to see what I'd do.

I slipped the doll into the diary box. Then I closed the flaps, tightly, and put it into the trunk.

Just as we were pulling out of the driveway, Grandma Kitty yelled, "*Stop!*" It made me nervous, even though I didn't think I was doing anything wrong. One time we had been driving into Canada, which is only a cough away from my grandparents' house. When they stop you at the border, they ask penetrating, important questions like, "Are you bringing any *fruit* with you?" and "What exactly *is* your business in Canada?" Even if you have no fruit and your business is shopping, it makes you feel paranoid. Like you want to confess to a stashed apple in the trunk and let them lead you to jail just to relieve your conscience.

"Can we go back?" Grandma asked. "I have something for Mary."

Dad drove back, trying hard not to roll his eyes, I could see. He cleared his throat several times. I slipped another peanut butter heart to him. He gobbled it in one bite.

G Kitty came back to the car—not stopping by the trunk, I might add—and we were on our way back to Planet Cancer.

Two hours later we pulled up and walked into the apartment. Grandma Kitty busied herself in the kitchen putting away groceries and scrubbing around the burners. I asked Tucker to help me unload the car.

"Can't you see I'm busy here?" he asked. In the corner, under the window and next to the African violet the previous occupants had left, Tucker was building a house out of playing cards.

I yanked his arm and whispered harshly into his ear as I dragged him toward the elevator. "And can't *you* see that Mom and Dad want some time alone before he goes back home?"

"Oh. I never thought of that." He straightened the collar of his sweat shirt and pulled it down over his jeans.

Right then and there I thought of a new list. I kept it in my head, for now. I was sure I could add to it later.

Reasons Quinn Is Glad She Is Not a Boy
#1 Bad clothing choices.
#2 Rather be a mom than a dad. No
      offense, Daddy.
#3 CLUELESS on the interpersonal
      relationship level. (Adam?)

The last one would have to remain a question mark. Adam was doing okay so far. He'd sent me a really nice email earlier, updating me on all of our friends and what was happening at school. On the bottom he'd pasted some knock-knock jokes. Corny. But what I'd needed.

"Would you take this?" I handed Grandma Kitty's suitcase to Tucker. I wanted to take the box in.

"Sure," Tucker said. He looked at me anxiously. "Do you think Mom and Dad have had enough time together? We could wait in the lobby."

I ruffled his hair. "Yeah." He was a good Joe. I was glad he was my brother. I decided not to write down the last list after all.

Dad left and Grandma Kitty got to cooking for the evening. Her hands looked kind of gnarled and red. "Can I help?" I asked.

She shooed me away. "No, thank you." I think she thought I would botch something up.

Note to self: *Look for fettuccine carbonara recipe online.*

After supper, Mom showered and packed her bag to take to treatment tomorrow. I went to kiss her goodnight.

"Did you get the box?" Mom asked.

I nodded. "And something else," I said. "A surprise." I'd kept them all back so we could share them at a private moment.

"Hey!" she laughed. "I was supposed to surprise *you.*"

"You did," I reassured her. I looked into the living room. No sign of G Kitty. Tucker was working on his card house. "I'll go and get the box from my room."

I went into my room. Grandma Kitty was listening to jazz in the kitchen and running reams of carrots through the Veggo, so she couldn't hear me. I grabbed the box and went back to Mom.

We sat cross-legged together on her bed like we always did. All of a sudden I started to cry.

Mom drew near. "What's the matter?"

"Who's going to sit on the bed with me after you go?"

She covered my hand with hers. "I'm here right now."

I wiped my face with the back of my hand. She wiped her tears, too. The storm passed, like hundreds before it and hundreds to come on Planet Cancer. You just never knew when they would hit. We were used to it by now.

"So show me what's in the box."

I fumbled the box open and drew the doll out. Mom's eyes got as big as Grandma Kitty's had earlier.

"*Where* did you find *that*?" she asked.

"Um, in the attic." I looked at her wide-eyed face. "I hope I didn't make a mistake in bringing her."

Mom reached out and took the doll in her hands. She smoothed the creases of the dress and wrapped the little red velvet purse strings around her thumb. "No, no mistake. I had thought she was gone all these years. I'm delighted. I thought she was thrown or given away."

"Why?"

Mom motioned for me to shut her door.

"Well," she started, "this was my childhood doll all the way till, I suppose, about fifth grade. I had given all the others away but kept her because she was so . . . so . . ."

"Chic?" I offered.

Mom nodded. "Yes! Chic. I mean, look at this dress! It's designer. And this little handbag. To die for."

I thought it was pretty cool, too.

"Anyway," Mom continued, "Grandma Kitty used to sew a lot of my clothes back then. For my birthday she said she'd make me whatever I wanted. Of course, I told her I wanted a red velvet dress just like this one. Grandma Kitty said no, it would be too hot out. It'd be inappropriate."

Mom's birthday was in June. This was a long-sleeved dress. "But if that's what you wanted. . . ?"

"She and I fought about it, and the more she said no the more I wanted it. Finally Grandpa took the doll and said if it was going to be that much of a problem he'd set her aside for a while."

"And you never got her back?"

"I just stopped thinking about her, I guess," Mom said. "Grandma Kitty and I made up. She made me a beautiful jean dress for my birthday. And I got lots of new stuff and I didn't play with dolls very much anyway, so we both kind of forgot. Grandma must have discovered it when she cleaned out the attic years ago. She saved her," Mom marveled.

"Well, she didn't want me to bring it today," I said.

"No wonder," Mom said. "Bad memories. Let's tuck her away." She opened a dresser drawer. "No sense bringing out hurt feelings right now. She's been a very good mother . . . most of the time."

"Like you," I teased. "Most of the time."

Mom threw a pillow at me. "You get to bed, girlie. I am going to look through these diaries for a surprise or two I have in mind. I want to give them to you tomorrow."

I kissed her cheek. She'd never even asked if I had read any of the diaries. I was so glad I'd kept her trust.

Grandma Kitty had cleaned up and was watching TV in the pullout bed she slept in. I kissed her cheek. By the side of her bed was a package neatly wrapped in tissue paper. "Is your mom asleep yet?" she asked.

I shook my head and helped G Kitty out of the bed. "I'll just bring this in, then," she said. She took the present she had gone back into the house to get. I had seen it. It was G Kitty's favorite, warmest lap blanket freshly pressed and wrapped.

I left them alone and went to my own room. Tucker had his earbuds in and was playing with his Game Boy Advance. He'd already kissed Mom good-night. Through the walls I heard Mom and G Kitty talking softly. Everyone wanted time alone with Mom. I had to remember that G Kitty was Mom's mom. I knew she did everything she could here to help her daughter— just like my mom would. Even the vile Veggo.

I went to sleep, too. *Thank you, Lord, for G Kitty,* I prayed before I fell into dreams.

The next morning, at school, I checked my email at break. There was a message from Adam.

Hey Quinn,
   Just thought I'd drop a note and tell you that

I'm doing okay. The semester is ending pretty soon and I'll have more time to write. Everything is going smooth for the Valentine's party. You're going to be back, right? Do you still want to be with us on the planning committee? I mean, it was your idea to get the youth involved, and we're all kind of carrying on what you started, but we're not sure what else to do. Email back some ideas, okay? We're meeting tonight.

Don't worry, I haven't let anyone take your place. The green beanbag is yours, girl.

Back to algebra.

G2G,
Adam

I wondered if he *just* meant he hadn't let anyone take my seat at youth group, where I always sat on the green beanbag in the Dungeon, where we met. Or if he *also* meant he wasn't going to let anyone take my *place*. With him.

Two hands clasped over my eyes from behind. "Coffee after school?"

It was Annie. I logged off of Yahoo.

"Well, I'm going up the hill because my mom is starting treatment again today." I had a wicked inspiration. "I'll come for coffee with you if you come on the hill with me." I knew her mom was starting week eight of treatment today.

She backed up and looked down. "Nah, we can go another day."

My heart dropped. Who was I to push her? "I can do coffee for a little while. Just let me walk Tucker home first."

She smiled. "Okay. I'll meet you there." Her hair was pulled back into a French braid.

"New 'do?"

She nodded. She had a pretty sweater on, too.

"You look great, and I need to go shopping," I said.

She giggled. I saw Ben walking toward us, so I made myself scarce.

After school I dragged Tucker down the hall. "Why do I have to stay home all afternoon with Grandma Kitty while you get to have fun?"

"Because you're ten and I'm not," I said. I needed to have him agree so there wouldn't be a fuss. "Do some cancer research on the computer for your note-books, and I'll bring something home for you, okay?"

He nodded sadly. "How about a theobroma lactose?"

"Huh?" I asked. "I'm not going to a lab."

"Hot chocolate," he said as he turned the doorknob of the apartment. "And a friend."

When I got into Starbucks, I saw Annie—she was

talking with Ben! I hung back. He nodded a hello to me and then headed up the hill.

"Well, *that* was convenient," I said. "I now see why the new 'do and nice sweater." I was all ready to get my hazelnut white chocolate mocha and cross off the first coffee on my list when Annie grinned and handed me a hot cup. "I saved our seats," she said, "and ordered a vanilla latte for you. Is that okay?"

Don't get me wrong, lists are *very* important to me. Linear, predictable, check it off. Like math. But friends are even more important. Vanilla latte was not on my list, but . . .

"Vanilla latte is fine," I said. "Thanks." We sat down together.

"Ben is going up the hill to visit his dad. His dad has to stay there full time for two more weeks because of transplants."

"Oh," I said. "I'd probably better go soon, too. But I have a few minutes." I didn't want her to think I was racing past our time together.

She didn't bring out her sewing. "So why do you guys even go there? I mean, it's just a nasty reminder of the cancer."

"The cancer is there whether you want it to be or not," I said. "Don't you guys ever talk about it at all?"

"We don't talk about much," Annie admitted. "I kind of want to, but we're not that kind of family. Mom told us she had cancer; we wanted to come here because Beth's family said it was the best. My dad arranged to work from home for three months, and here we are.

"My mom was very sick from treatment all these weeks," she continued. "Hot flashes, mood swings, hair loss. It's a hard experience for me to see my mom in such pain."

"Does she want to talk? Or does she prefer to do that with your dad?"

Annie laughed. "No. My parents were on the verge of a divorce when this came up. I think my dad felt bad going through with it when she got sick, but who knows when it's over."

Wow. I had nothing to say for once. I wondered why they wanted to divorce, but I didn't ask.

Annie grew soft. "Strangely, this seems to have changed things somehow."

I nodded. "Cancer does that. I'll pray for you."

Annie looked startled. "Thanks. No one has ever said that to me before. My mom will get better, anyway."

I wrestled with that. It was true—her mom would probably never get worse than stage two. Most women didn't. My mom was one of the unfortunate exceptions.

I checked my watch. "I'd better get up on the hill.

Do you want to meet tonight after dinner? Do homework in the rec room?"

She brightened. "Yeah. I'll help you with geography if you help me with math."

I laughed. "You've already noticed my weak spot!"

"And your strength, too!" she said.

I nodded. "See you then."

Walking up the hill to the hospital took about ten minutes, but I was glad for the time because it gave me a chance to switch gears from teenager to caretaker. I talked to God about Annie. I talked to God about me. I talked to God about my mom. Then I was there. In Leavenworth I always stopped at the pop machine on the main floor and got a Gatorade before heading up to see my mom. I drank it for twelve weeks, all through the first chemo. I hate Gatorade now. It smells like sickness.

I looked at the names on the fifth floor. Mercy Meyer's name was on the first door I came to—Annie's mom! I heard a man's voice talking quietly. Annie's dad? Three doors down was Mom.

I tapped lightly. Mom was holding on to the bedrail, ready to climb in. "Bed this time?" I asked.

"I felt a little unsteady," she said. "Maybe just tired. I thought a bed would be better than a chair today."

Panic filled my throat, sour and unwelcome. I swallowed it down. "Well, I'll read to you or something, okay?"

She climbed in and smiled. "No, no, I'm going to get some rest. First, though, I found something for you."

She leaned over to the diaries on the table by the side of her bed and reached into the inside cover of one. "Lists!" she said.

I looked longingly at the diaries. I wondered if I'd ever read them or if they were just between Mom and God.

There was a small sheaf of four or five papers in her hand. She opened one and read it. "'Mary's New Year's Resolutions!

"'Quit eating candy.'"

I snorted and laughed along with her. "You didn't keep it, I hope."

Mom laughed out loud and popped a conversation heart from the large bag I had given her last week. "Nope!"

"'Get a purple room'" was next.

"Got it," I said, thinking of the chenille bedspread. "Next?"

"'Replace Andy Gibb poster.'"

"Andy *who*?" I asked. Mom just giggled.

We read over a few more lists, all but the last one, and then she handed them all to me, folded over. "See how alike we are? You didn't even know I wrote lists. And I never even suggested that you do them."

I nodded. We were so alike. I loved it when people noticed. Mom closed her eyes and we chatted for just a little while. When she was sleeping soundly, I rearranged some candy hearts on her table so they read "I Love You" and "Call Me" and "Smile." Then I took the lists and headed out to buy a theobroma lactose for Tucker and a soy latte for G Kitty.

I read the last list on the way down the hill. Now I know why she didn't read it out loud to me but let me read it in private. I read it and cried. *I love my mommy, Jesus. Please let her stay with me for a while longer. You don't need her. I do.*

Mary's List of Things to Do Before I Die
(in 80 years that is)

#1 Fly a plane
#2 Kiss a boy
#3 Bake homemade bread
#4 Dance the Hustle (okay, I know disco is out, but still)
#5 Start my own business
#6 Have a daughter

CHAPTER FOUR

Tucker and I walked down the hallway toward our apartment. It was Wednesday. The school week was half over. Of course, it didn't hurt that Fitzschool was only from nine to twelve-thirty. A nice perk, but I'd rather have been home in Leavenworth.

I opened the door to our apartment, but no one was in there. Not Mom. Not Grandma Kitty. "What's up?" I asked Tucker.

"Debbie and Dana came, remember?" he said.

"And Grandma Kitty went to lunch with her friend Mabel."

"Why aren't Debbie and Dana here, then?" I asked. "Mom was probably tired today after treatment. I don't think she went anywhere."

"They can't come into the apartment," Tucker reminded me. The rule was no visitors on the apartment levels in case someone was sick and could spread a virus or whatever.

"They're probably downstairs." I tossed my backpack into the living room and headed back down to the lobby, a different direction from the hallway that led from school. When I got there, I saw that the volunteer staff was setting out pastries. It was nice they did so much. Every little bit helped.

Sure enough, all three—Mom, Debbie, and Dana—sat together on the leather couch, giggling. I stood back a minute, watching. Whenever my mom was in treatment, her skin got really thin. Sometimes it made her mouth break out and sometimes it made her hands and feet burn so bad she had to put them into a bucket of water. When she had the chemo that Annie's mom was having, her fingernails fell off.

Not this time. But her skin still had that thin, white glow. Kind of like an angel.

"There she is!" Mom's face broke out into a smile. I hugged Debbie tightly but just gave a celebrity hug to

Dana. Who knew what she'd been asking Mom while we were away? Dana was nibbling on a pastry.

"Dana was just asking if you guys wanted to go into Seattle with them this afternoon. She's got some things to pick up downtown, and she brought CJ with her to visit with Tucker." I hadn't noticed Tucker's friend off to the side, reading a comic book.

"Sure," I said. What was I going to do with two boys and two women downtown?

Round Two: Dana.

But actually, it was a nice thing to do. I could bring Tucker his hot chocolate, but only Dana could bring him his friend.

"Would you like to ask Annie to go along?" Mom said.

I nodded. "Yes. I'll call her."

"We'll meet you outside in a few minutes," Dana said. I smiled back at her, warmly this time.

Mom and I hurried upstairs—at least, as much as Mom *could* hurry—to tell Tucker, who slowly backed away from his house of cards so it wouldn't collapse. "That's great. Doctor *Domino*!" CJ was the domino master. Tucker break-danced on the floor.

"Wow, Tuck, I didn't know you could do that," I said.

"There's a lot you don't know about me." He arched his eyebrow and we both laughed.

Mom said nothing, just kind of bustled around the apartment getting our coats ready. She thrust mine at me. "Hurry up and call Annie," she said. She seemed somehow different than she'd been down-stairs just a minute ago. Like she was trying to get rid of us. Pushy.

Annie answered on the first ring. "I am only *too* happy to get out of the house. My mom has been so sick she hasn't been out of bed for two days, and I have to keep quiet. Dad works on the computer all day." We agreed to meet downstairs. I grabbed a Nerds Rope and propelled Tucker toward the door.

"Hey!" I said, meeting up with Annie before we went out to meet with Debbie, Dana, and CJ. "Oh, wait a minute." I dug into my purse and took out my wallet. I only had like fifteen dollars in it. That wasn't going to do it. "I didn't bring enough money. I can't remember if there's someplace to buy clothes, but if there is I want to pick up a shirt or something. I'll be right back."

Annie and Tucker agreed to meet me at the van.

I ran up the stairs, but as soon as I got to our door, I could hear my mom crying. Not weeping softly, but sobbing and talking really loud. "*Why* can't I just be allowed to finish what I start? I am not asking for any-thing big. Why let me get involved and enjoy it and then have to quit? Why take that away from someone who has nothing?" I heard footsteps as she walked toward her bedroom.

Who is she talking to? Herself? What is she angry about?

I steadied my hand on the knob. *God, what should I do?* I wanted to shove the door open and comfort my mom. But Annie was waiting in the car, on my invitation, with people she didn't know. In reality, my mom had tried to shoo us out of the apartment. She hadn't wanted me there. I guess she wanted some time alone.

I backed away from the door. I'd buy clothes another day.

I took the steps down, heavily now. Inside I wanted to stay. I wanted to comfort her or call Grandma Kitty or Dad to do it or *something*. Instead, I tried really hard to paint a pink pouty smile on myself so I didn't ruin it for everyone else downtown. Especially Tucker, who finally had a friend with him.

Dana had better not have said anything stupid again.

The drive to Seattle Center was quick—it was only a few miles away. Seattle Center has some cool stores, but it's much more than a shopping center. It's this great place that has something for everyone—the Pacific Science Center, an opera house, a children's theater, the Key Arena for basketball, a huge fountain for little kids to swim in . . . and a food court. Yum.

"Would you girls like to walk around while we take the boys to the science area?" Debbie asked.

"Yeah, thanks," I said. She told us when to meet them back at the entrance, and we promised we would. I kept my cell phone on, for safety.

We wandered around for a while, looking at some shops, the opera house, the theater. We sat on the moist lawn and chitchatted about boys and school and anything except breast cancer. I pushed my mom's situation out of my mind—to keep my sanity. My stomach growled.

"Hey, I haven't eaten lunch yet. I didn't bring one to class again. Have you eaten?" I asked Annie.

She shook her head. "I wasn't hungry before."

I sighed.

"What's the matter?" she said as we walked to the middle of the Seattle Center House, which held the world's largest food court. Or so it seemed.

"This is going to take some of my money," I said. "I was hoping to buy some clothes. Like yours." I gestured toward her peach button-up shirt over a white T-shirt and slim-fitting khakis.

She giggled. "You can't buy this shirt."

"You bought it in Olathe?"

She shook her head. "I made it."

I sighed again. Twice.

We bought Indian food and shared it. "Want dessert?"

"Oh yeah." The Nerds Rope was long gone.

I had spied some elephant ears when we first walked in. I ordered one—I mean, it must have been a huge elephant because the ear was, like, one foot around, sanded with cinnamon sugar and hot raspberry jam.

I took it, smoking hot, back to our table.

"Now, that's what I'm talking about," Annie said. We dug in, tearing off a piece at a time. It was so sweet, I needed something to drink to wash it down.

"Want some coffee?" I asked.

She nodded.

"Double espresso, straight up?" I asked.

She opened her eyes wide and smiled. "Sure."

Quinn's List of Drinks I Must Have While
in Seattle, Before My Starbucks Card
Runs Out of Credit

#1 Hazelnut white chocolate mocha with
   extra whipped cream
#2 Green Tazo tea with two packs of raw
   sugar
#3 Chantico Drinking Chocolate
#4 Double espresso. Straight up.

Our barista was a girl only a few years older than we were. Asian. Annie was practically twitching. I was going to ask her about it this time.

We bought the coffee and strolled outside, pausing by the huge fountain.

"So, you don't have many Asian Americans in Olathe?" I asked. I mean, who knows? Kansas was a long ways away.

Annie looked puzzled. "Um, I don't know. That's a weird question."

I sipped my hot coffee, pretending that the heat didn't scorch my tongue and that I didn't hate the bitter taste—like aspirin—on my lips. "I just noticed a couple of times that you kind of freak out when any Asian girls are around."

The day was cool and a cloud floated overhead. Some younger kids squealed with laughter as they tossed plastic balls into the fountain. The balls floated right back to them like bouncy boomerangs.

"My sister is Korean," Annie finally said. She seemed a little jumpy. Maybe it was all that caffeine.

"Well, cool. I didn't know you had a sister. How come she isn't here?" I asked.

"She lives in Korea."

"Oh, well . . ." I didn't know what else to say. "What is she like?"

"I don't know." Annie tossed back the rest of her

coffee—she didn't even wince. But her hand was shaking. "We've never met."

I sat there. I do talk a lot, in general, but I also know when to shut up.

"Right before my mom got sick, my dad got this letter from a girl—or woman, I guess, she's nineteen—named Sun-Hea. She said she's my dad's daughter. And she wants to come and visit him this summer when she's in the U.S."

"And—you knew nothing about her?"

"Nope. Neither did my mom."

"Oh, I see." Bad news. Bad secret.

"My dad knew he had a daughter—from a relationship he had when he was in the army before my parents met. But Sun-Hea's mom had wanted nothing more to do with him. He lost touch. He married my mom. He kept it to himself."

I checked my watch and stood up. I hated to interrupt her, but we needed to get back to meet Debbie and Dana and the boys.

"Is that why they were getting a divorce?"

"I think it was the last straw," Annie said. "Then my mom got sick. We never talked about it again. But Sun-Hea has to pay for her plane tickets by March 1, so she's asked my dad to tell her by then. She's coming one way or another—the question is, will she visit us or not?"

"What are they going to do?"

"I think they were so overwhelmed with the sickness that it kind of got forgotten. My mom was really warming to the whole idea—wondering where Sun-Hea could sleep if she visited and all—but hadn't talked about it with Dad. Dad said nothing. He didn't want to upset my mom further, and I can understand that. But he keeps Sun-Hea's letters and emails all together in a little envelope by his computer. I've seen it."

Annie tossed her cup in the garbage and ran her fingers through her hair. "I'm not used to sharing my parents. But I always wanted a sister. Dad forwarded one email from Sun-Hea that said she wanted to meet *me*! But of course, no one has decided anything. And March is coming."

I nodded. I had nothing else to say. Just then I caught sight of Dana out of the corner of my eye—waving toward us. "Uh-oh, better run," I said.

We caught up with them and got in the middle seats of the van. In the backseat CJ and Tucker pestered each other like the boys they were, sliming each other with some chemical concoction they had bought at the science center. Annie and I just sat together.

"I can make you a shirt," she said on the way back. "If we can find a sewing machine."

I smiled. "Thanks. I'd like that."

When we opened the door to the apartment, G Kitty was humming over hummus—I'm not kidding. It was Middle Eastern health food tonight, folks. Good thing I'd eaten lunch at the food court.

Mom was napping—maybe worn out from emotions. I took out my notebook, into which I had copied her last list. We hadn't had a chance to talk about it at all yet. She'd fallen asleep at treatment on Monday before I read it, and today she just came home in time to see Debbie and Dana. I read it again.

What's the Hustle?

I logged onto Yahoo and tried to steel my stomach to eat the hummus in a few minutes.

Dear Dad,
How was your day? Are you sleeping okay? Do you have any children we don't know about?

I erased that last line. Seriously, I felt bad for Annie, even though it would be great to have a long lost sister. *Lord, please help them to make the right decision. Help her mom to get well. Help her parents to stay together. It would really stink to think you might lose your mom but even if you didn't your family could bust up.*

Dear Dad,

How was your day? Are you sleeping okay? I want to ask you a question. What is the Hustle? I mean, it's a kind of dance, I know, but what? Have you ever danced it? Has Mom? Will you be back here on Friday? If you get this before church tonight and you see the Maxwells, ask them how Velveeta is doing. I miss you.

Love,
Tiger Lily

Hey Adam,

Whazzup? We are all fine here. I had a good day with my friend Annie. We hung out at Seattle Center. Very cool, but I'd rather be home. I'm sending an attachment of my ideas for the youth part of the Valentine's party. All you have to do is get it set up. Marcie will help you. She's great. Just don't get too used to working together. Ha-ha. I can take care of the rest when we get home. I'll be back a couple of days before the party. Save my bean bag and my Moose Munch.

TTYL,
Q

I wasn't going to write *Love, Quinn.* Or, *Save your heart for me.*

Life was going on without me in Leavenworth.

We sat down for dinner. You know what? The hummus was good, especially when followed by a Cadbury Creme Egg. My mom made it to the table, and she'd even pulled her hair back in a claw. If you hadn't known that she'd been crying earlier in the day, you'd never have noticed. I knew, though. I noticed. I was going to ask her about it after G Kitty went to bed. Grandma Kitty cleared the table and shooed us out of the room before giving Mom a manicure and hand massage. It was one thing that soothed Mom when she didn't feel good.

Later on I opened the window in the living room. It was a rare Seattle evening, no rain, just a cool breeze washing my face and cooling the sweat on my brow. Mom was in the shower. G Kitty was watching TV from the pullout.

"What are you doing?" I asked Tucker. "You need to get ready for bed."

"I'm working on my card house," he said. He placed the cards one by one, steadying his hand and making sure the heater on the floor was turned off so no air would blow by.

"Did you do any research today?" I asked.

He nodded and his eyes filled with tears. Whoa! I was just trying to find something to make him feel good.

free my hand to help her. Everything fell out of it.

She nodded. "My legs must have fallen asleep or something." I helped her back to the couch and then went to scoop up the stuff that had fallen out of my purse. Mom leaned over to help me. She grabbed my lip gloss and handed it over, then my notebook, which had fallen open.

"Is that your New Year's resolutions list?" Mom asked. "The one you had in my room this week?"

I nodded. She didn't ask, but I wanted to offer. Suddenly I wanted to share everything with my mom. Not hide anything. I wanted her to know me. "Do you want to see them?"

She sat back. "Do you *want* me to see them?"

I nodded and sat next to her. She opened up the journal.

Quinn's New Year's Resolutions

#1 Help mom stay healthy.

#2 Drive a car before any of my friends. I am not kidding. Otherwise I will ONCE AGAIN be last since all my friends will turn 15 before I do. I just want to be first, at one thing that is important, for once.

#3 Make an unhealthy meal that Grandma Kitty says tastes delicious.

#4 Get kissed by a boy. Not Tucker.

"What did you find out?" I asked.

"NOTHING!" he practically shouted. "And don't go looking in my notebooks, either."

I shook it off. He wiped his hand across his cheek and went back to work. I went into our bedroom and stared at his notebooks. He was in the living room. He'd never know. I started walking toward them. *What did he find out?*

"Quinn?" Mom called from the other bedroom. "Come in for a few minutes while I'm awake and tell me about your day."

I went into her room and sat on her bed, cross-legged. "We had a good time at Seattle Center," I told her. Should I tell her about Annie's sister? Annie hadn't said I could. I'd better not.

"I think Annie needs some time away," Mom said. "They've had a hard time." Mom didn't say anything to me if she knew.

"Mom?"

She kissed my forehead. "Yes?"

"I heard you crying today. I came back to get some money and heard you through the door. Are you okay?"

Mom sighed. "Yes. I'm okay. Dana told me some news about Ribbons in the Snow."

"Isn't it doing okay?"

"It's doing great. They are making tons of money.

Lots of people have signed up to ski in the event. More money is being made for breast cancer research than ever before. They have a fantastic speaker and terrific food, and it's going to be the best time ever."

"So why are you upset?"

"I started it and I won't be there. I care so much about it, I put it into motion, and now I won't even be there. I can't run the risk of the pass icing over and my not being able to get back here again," Mom sniffled.

"You've done a lot of hard work for that." I stood up and went to get my mom's soft boar bristle brush off her dresser. I brought it back and sat behind her and brushed her hair. We had always brushed each other's hair; it was one of the things we'd missed most when her hair was gone. "Everyone knows you did it all, Mom."

"Oooh, that feels good," she said, then sighed. "I just want to see it all come to be."

"You'll be there next year," I encouraged.

Mom said nothing. I kept brushing. After a few minutes she said, "The truest test of a work is if the values hold fast and the program grows even when you're not there."

"Sometimes Dana bugs me," I said. "She never brings good news."

"She asked if you wanted to go to the Seattle Center," Mom pointed out. "And she invited you and

Tucker to go back the weekend after this one for Ribbons in the Snow."

I jumped up. "*Really?*" Then I sat back down. "But won't you miss me?"

Mom smiled. "Of course. But a weekend alone with Daddy will be nice, too."

I set the brush down. "That's probably what Annie's parents could use, too. If she wasn't there, maybe they'd have to talk."

"Quinn, you can't force other people to talk."

"I know."

"But you can invite Annie." Mom's eyes sparkled. "Her mom should be feeling a bit better by the weekend. Maybe they'd like some time alone."

"Did Dana say it's okay for Annie to come?"

"Yes, she did. She's really nice, Quinn. She's been a good friend to me."

I knew she had. When Mom had her first chemo, Dana went with her every week, 'cause Tucker and I were at school and Dad was at work. She picked Mom up and brought special whole wheat treats and sugarless candy worms. When all the other patients had left, Mom had to stay since her chemo was tougher. Dana would take a lounge chair, too, and do Bible study with my mom so she could keep up with her group at church.

I kissed Mom's cheek. "Love you. See you in the morning?"

She nodded. "If I can wake up that early. Otherwise I'll see you after school."

I went back into the living room. "You'd better say good-night to Mom if you want to," I said. "She looks tired."

"Does she have circles under her eyes? Were her words slurred? Did she seem unsteady again?"

I just looked at him. "No. Why?"

He shook his head. "Nothing. I'm going to say good-night."

Okay. Whatever.

G Kitty sat reading a magazine, and I went over and logged on to the computer. There were two emails!

Hey there,

  I got the attachment for the party, but I'm not sure about what to do. I will call Marcie and we'll get together and figure it out. Thanks again!

  G2G,

  Adam

Well, that was pretty short, to the point and businesslike. Was it just regular guy talk? Or was I losing out to someone else?

I clicked on email number two. Dad.

Hey, Tiger Lily,

Why do you want to know what the Hustle is?
It's a dance, a disco dance, so I can guess where
you heard about it—something having to do with
Mom. No, I don't believe she's ever danced it since
it would have to have been with me and I have
never danced it.

Then Dad had inserted two figures. A nice-looking
man, and a man in a chicken suit, animated, clicking
across the email.

The first one was labeled *Me,* and the second one,
Me dancing.

"*See you on Friday,*" he said and signed off. "*Love,*
Dad."

I wrote back right away.

The Valentine's dance is coming up in a few
weeks. You know, where you're supposed to dance?
I got a list from Mom of things she wanted to do,
and dancing the Hustle was one of the things.
Think about it.

I sat there thinking for a while. Why didn't I want
to send it? Wouldn't Mom be excited to dance the Hustle? She'd put it on her list! What bugged me? Probably
something stupid. I clicked Send and sent it off.

Tucker came out, looking glum. He closed Mom's door, and the swoosh of air that came with it made his house of cards fall down.

"Oh no! It's ruined!"

"It's okay. I'll help you build it up again."

"That's not what I mean." He went in to our room. "I never want to do a card house again, anyway. They're a waste of time."

What did he mean? I followed him and sat down on my bed.

I prayed for a minute. All of a sudden my eyes flew open.

Is that why she gave the list to me? If I helped her do all the things she wanted to do, would I be helping her to finish what she wanted to accomplish or would I be giving her permission to die? If Dad did the Hustle, what would be left? I opened my desk drawer and slipped out my journal. I didn't want to mark up my mom's handwritten list, so I had copied it into my notebook before crossing things off. Tucker wasn't even paying attention, so that was good. I didn't have to tell him.

"I'm going to the bathroom to change," I said, burying the list inside of my pajamas. I went into the bathroom, turned the water on for privacy, and sat down on the cold, closed toilet lid. Then I opened the book up again and drew a line through the things on the list I knew she'd done.

Two left. One if Dad followed up on my email.

Mary's List of Things to Do Before I Die
(in 80 years that is)

#1 Fly a plane

#2 ~~Kiss a boy~~

#3 ~~Bake homemade bread~~

#4 Dance the Hustle (okay, I know disco is out,
    but still)

#5 ~~Start my own business~~

#6 ~~Have a daughter~~

CHAPTER FIVE

O kay, feel this bolt.''
Annie held a big wrap of fabric out to
me.

"Bolt? Like lightning?" I laughed. "I'll feel it but
I have no idea what it is that I'm looking for." I
reached my hand out and slipped it between two
folds of cotton. It felt cool and silky against my
skin, like fresh bed sheets. "Ooh, awesome."

Annie smiled. "See? You do know what you're
looking for." She wheeled the cart down the row.

"I think you look good in mauve. Wine colors. Sophisticated."

I hurried to catch up with her as she tossed several more bolts into the cart for me to look at. The store was packed on a Sunday afternoon, so I had to weave through customers. "You really do? Sophisticated colors?"

"Yep. I've always envied that about dark-haired girls. I can't carry dark colors. I look like bride of Frankenstein."

"Well, I look like a yellow-skinned lizard in the light colors you can wear," I said. Secretly, I was glad she thought I looked good in sophisticated colors.

"I don't suppose this can be ready by Friday." Five days till our weekend in Leavenworth.

She stopped the cart dead in the aisle. "This isn't slave labor, you know."

I elbowed her. "Seriously, I am so glad you offered to do this. The big shocker is that G Kitty is going to bring down her dressmaker's thingamabob and sewing machine tonight."

"Your grandma seems nice," Annie said. "I like that lunch she packed for you."

"Pita-spinach roll-ups? With goat cheese?"

"Mm-hmm," Annie said. She tossed a plastic case of pins into the cart. "Healthy."

That gave me the willies. I reached into my purse

and pulled out a mini Snickers. "Want one?"

She shook her head. "No. I'm swearing off candy."

Oh.

"Since yesterday," she said, as if reading my mind. I mean, she *had* eaten a whole Nerds Rope with me a few days ago. I decided to let it pass. For now.

"So what *should* I wear on Friday?" I asked.

"Remind me, what is Friday?" Annie threw a tape measure into the cart.

"What is *that* for?"

"Your measurements. We can't very well make the shirt without taking your measurements."

Just great. What measurements? "On Friday we're going to a get-together at my church. There will be a lot of people hanging out, playing foosball and pinball and eating pizza and listening to music and stuff. We have a lot of old couches and a cool music system in the Dungeon."

"Dungeon?"

"The youth have the whole basement. It's cool. Trust me."

"Are you sure your friends will want me there?"

"Oh yeah," I said. "They'll be totally glad to hang out with you."

I wondered if Adam preferred dark sophisticates to pretty blondes. Hmm.

"You can borrow a sweater if you want," Annie said.

"I have a chocolate brown one that would look really good on you. And you should definitely wear those button-up boots. They are so cool."

Chocolate brown. Okay. We rounded the corner to an aisle with a sign that said Notions.

"What are notions?" I asked. "Like commotion? Locomotion? Lotion?"

"No," she laughed. "Buttons and stuff. Which fabric do you like best?"

I looked at the cotton bolts and picked one that was a true, deep cranberry with a satin thread throughout it. Annie nodded her approval. "Me too. We'd better get going. My dad looks bored."

I strained to see the front of the store. Annie's dad sat on a chair, drinking a cup of stale coffee. "It was nice of him to bring us," I said.

"Yeah," she answered. "It was. My mom is sleeping. Again. Her mouth is so broken out in sores from chemo that she can't eat anything or even talk."

"Are they okay with your coming with me on Friday?"

"Yeah. I'm thinking about leaving a letter for my parents to read—together—while I am in Leavenworth with you. I just don't know if I should do it yet. First I'd have to send an email."

To her parents? I wanted to ask her what it was going to say and give her my undiluted opinion that they needed to talk more and she should encourage it. But she got that closed-mouth look and handed three bolts of fabric to me. "Will you bring these back so I can get the buttons?" She spoke before I could say anything else.

Obediently, I took the fabric bolts and headed back a row while she picked out the notions. I set them back with the other wine-colored fabric, and as I did I passed a whole row of luxury fabric. I slipped my hand between the folds again.

Then, one row over, I saw it.

An entire bolt of red velvet. A couple of women were standing next to it, but I was aching to slip my hand between the soft folds of it. So I kind of hung out, waiting. And eavesdropping, a little. But I couldn't help it! It's a public place!

"Should we buy it now?" the older lady asked. Okay, she wasn't *older*. She was probably five years older than my mom. Mom would kill me if she thought I called her an older lady.

"Yes, let's," the young woman in her twenties said. "I know the awards banquet isn't till March, but this kind of fabric might sell out before Valentine's Day."

They took the bolt with them before I could touch it. It was the exact shade of red velvet as on the doll hiding in my mom's drawer at Anderson House.

I looked up and saw Annie waving at me from the

notions aisle. I hurried over. She held up some ribbon and some buttons. "Like them?"

I nodded. "Very cool."

She threw some prepackaged fabric into the cart. "For head wraps. When I'm done with your shirt. Ready?"

"Ready," I said. We pushed the cart to the fabric cutting section. The women ahead of us had the red velvet.

"That's a beautiful fabric." Annie pointed at the red velvet as she turned toward me. "Hard to work with, though. It doesn't always cut or fold right. You have to cut it all in the same direction, every single piece; otherwise it looks funky when it's sewed together. You have to use a walking foot when you sew because it stretches. Easy to make a mistake that can't be fixed, and then it looks like junk."

"Walking foot?" I asked. "Is that a notion?" See, I had the vocabulary down pat.

"No, it's part of the machine." Annie grinned at me like an indulgent mother at a toddler. Or as a good friend to a good friend.

It made me feel like we really were good friends now.

At the checkout line I piled everything up and threw in a pack of playing cards and a book that said "509 Card Tricks!" on the packaging.

"Hey, those are mine!" Annie reached for the pre-packaged fabric pieces. "I'll pay for that."

"No way," I said. "It's the very least I can do."

"You're taking me with you this weekend," she said. "Getting me out. That's enough for me."

I firmly moved her toward the end of the line and paid for it all.

Annie's dad tried to make polite conversation all the way back to Anderson House. He was a good guy, but he looked really tired and beat up, like other husbands on Planet Cancer. I wondered if he played computer games in the middle of the night or cried at three in the morning.

When we got home, it wasn't that late, but my dad's car was gone. I felt a pit in my heart. I had thought he would stay till I came back.

"Daddy left?" I said as I came into the apartment.

"It's a long drive, Tiger Lily," Mom said. "He doesn't want to be driving on the ice when he's tired. We don't want him to, either, do we?"

I shook my head.

Mom looked at me. "He told me to tell you he'd 'hustle on back' this weekend. Exactly those words." She looked puzzled. She obviously had not made the connection between her list and what Dad had said. Maybe she'd forgotten. I'd noticed this treatment made her a little forgetful. When I'd told Tucker that, he'd clammed up.

I heard a knock on the door. It was Annie.

"Hey!"

She handed the cards and card trick book to me. "You left these in the bag."

I pocketed them for a surprise for later. I didn't want anyone to see.

She peered around the door. "Hey! A dummy!"

Tucker's mouth dropped open and my mom kind of smiled in an uncertain way. Only G Kitty laughed. "Yes, I brought it. And the sewing machine."

"I get it," I said. "The dressmaker's dummy."

Annie nodded. "Can we take these back to my apartment?" She wasn't supposed to come in, and I wasn't supposed to go into hers, but I thought I could tiptoe in and carry the machine with her. For just a minute.

"I'm going to take a bath," Mom said. G Kitty turned the jazz back on and started measuring the ingredients for sprouted bread. Tucker disappeared into our room, glum, notebook clamped under his arm.

Annie and I carried the dummy down the hall. It was kind of like a model, at least from the neck to the knees. "It holds the shirt or whatever on it while I'm pinning and working," Annie said. "I hope your grandmother doesn't miss it."

"She can't sew much anymore," I said. "A little hemming or a button here and there. That's all. She's got bad arthritis. I think she always hoped I would sew, but I don't."

When we'd maneuvered the dummy into Annie's apartment, we went back for the sewing machine.

"Do you want me to measure you tonight?" Annie asked as we found a spot for the machine. "I can make the notes then and get started this week when my mom heads back up the hill for treatment."

My mom was going too—week three out of four for my mom, week nine out of twelve for Annie's. "What do I need to do for you to measure me?" I asked.

"Just go get a tight-fitting T-shirt or something on, and then come back," Annie said. Her dad and mom were in their bedroom with the door shut, so I hoped it'd be okay that I was in their apartment.

"I'll be right back." I ran down to our apartment. Mom was still in the bathtub. No T-shirts in my drawer. Probably because G Kitty had been gone all weekend. She didn't want us to help her with the laundry. I think she sometimes felt so sad that keeping busy and helpful was the only way she could cope.

I tiptoed into Mom's room and opened her drawer.

She'd never minded when I borrowed clothes at home. T-shirts anywhere? I dug through and found . . . her prosthetic bra.

I pulled it out. When I was younger we had a name for girls who wadded up tissue and put it into their bras: stuffers. I think if the potential shame of discovery hadn't been so bad I might have been tempted.

That was different from the prosthetic bras, of course. These were the special bras that women wore after they'd had to have their breasts surgically removed because of cancer. My mom had had a full double mastectomy. Both breasts removed. We had thought at that time that it meant the cancer was gone for sure. It hadn't, as we found out a couple of years later.

This bra, though, had breast forms in it so that when Mom wore a shirt over it she looked like she had before the surgery. Mom even had a swimsuit like that. She didn't swim much anymore, though. Too tired from treatments.

I found a T-shirt and put it on. Sigh. I was still kind of . . . flat.

I suddenly had an inspiration. Mom wouldn't mind, would she?

I slipped out of the T-shirt, took my own bra off, and strapped on the prosthetic bra. Then I pulled the T-shirt over it. Wow! Talk about instant fill-out.

I pulled a big jacket over myself, snuck out, and slipped down to Annie's apartment again. I knocked on the door.

"Ready?" she asked.

I nodded. Her parents were still in the bedroom, apparently, because they were nowhere to be seen.

I took the jacket off. "Ready!" I announced.

She stared at me. "What happened to *you*? Balloons?"

I burst out laughing. "No, my mom's prosthetic bra. You don't think I should wear it?" I teased.

"I think people would notice the, uh, sudden eruption," she said. "Wait—I'll be right back."

She shooed me to the living room and disappeared into the bathroom. What if her parents came out *now*? I reached for the jacket and threw it on. I heard a drawer open and shut. A few minutes later she came out. Expanded.

"My mom has a prosthetic bra, too," she said. "She'll probably have reconstructive surgery, but not till after the chemo."

We looked at ourselves in the mirror, arm in arm. Then we burst out laughing.

Annie nodded. "You make me laugh. I never thought I could talk about cancer. *Laugh* about cancer. But I can, with you."

"We were meant to be friends," I said. "Flat or otherwise."

We sat there, admiring ourselves for a minute. "Do you ever worry that you'll get cancer, too?" I asked Annie.

She nodded. "But I've been too afraid to say it out loud. You know, when your mom gets it, it means you have a bigger chance of getting it yourself." She looked down. "I've just been afraid to say that out loud."

"Saying it out loud won't make it happen," I reassured her. "But I worry, too."

"That's why I'm not eating candy anymore." Annie looked toward her parents' bedroom. "My mom ate a lot of fast food."

A-ha. "My mom was a skier, an athlete, and she ate all of Grandma Kitty's health potions. But she still got breast cancer. It's good to be healthy, but just because you get it, it doesn't mean you necessarily did anything wrong."

"I know," she said. "I didn't draw the line at caffeine."

"You want to know why I eat candy?"

"You like sweets," Annie offered.

"Well, there is that," I agreed. "But also because I hope that when I grow up I become a Cinnamon Red Hot."

"Oh, does that work? I might start eating candy again," Annie said.

"I don't know. I'm worried I might actually be a Nerd. Or that people might Snicker."

"You're hopeless. And I don't know how you stay so thin eating candy all the time."

G Kitty did things to feel useful. Dad played computer games. Tucker tried research. I ate candy. "I'd better go and change," I said. "To get the real—if sadder—measurements."

I slid back down the hall like a lizard trying to avoid a cat, tiptoeing back into the apartment. Grandma Kitty was still kneading whole grains. I left the bra on and sat on my mom's bed, waiting for her before running back to Annie's.

When she came back in I stood up and pushed my chest out.

"Quinn!" she said just before I slammed the door shut so Tucker and G Kitty wouldn't come running. Then we both fell on the bed and laughed till I thought I'd have to run to the bathroom.

We overslept a little the next morning and Tucker and I had to race down the hall to class.

We spent a lot of time on math on Mondays. I was caught up with the stuff at home and was ready to move beyond algebra, but that was going to have to wait for ninth grade. Around midmorning we met in the social worker's office for group, and then we had free study time until lunch.

I liked the Monday counseling sessions, probably because I was okay talking about problems. Annie hated it. She didn't want to talk—and almost never did. But I knew she was listening. I tried to bring up things in group about myself that I thought would help her, too. We all had to go, though, like it or not.

"Can you help me with this?" Annie brought her own math over after group and sat next to me during free study time.

We spread her papers out, but Annie seemed unfocused. She looked down toward the table.

"Are you okay?"

"I guess so," she said. "My mom never even felt better this whole weekend. She has nothing to look forward to. It's not like she gets encouraging emails every day like your mom does."

"I'm sorry," I said. I didn't know what else to say. I never thought I'd think this, but right then I wished for a Dana for Annie's mom. A friend to care and walk through cancer with her.

We worked through Annie's math problems with help from *hotmath.com* and then turned to social studies.

The school was going on a field trip to a local park in the afternoon. "I'm sorry I can't come on the field trip," I said as we packed up our books. "I don't want to let you down, but I know you can hang with those guys." I pointed to the fun sisters—I'd come to refer to the older high school girls I'd originally made friends with that way. Sometimes Annie and I ate lunch with them or did our hair together at breaks.

"Nah, I'm not going."

Wow. Annie usually took every opportunity to get out of Anderson House.

"Well, do you want to stop for coffee before I head up the hill?" I asked.

She nodded.

I went to say good-bye to Tucker. He was downstairs dinking around on one of the computers, as usual, with the same friend I'd seen him with last week. I drew him aside.

"Going to be okay this afternoon?" I asked.

He nodded. "Frankie is coming on the field trip, too." He motioned to the other boy. "He likes science."

Tucker looked up at me. I noticed the dark circles

under his eyes for the first time.

"I'll tell Mom you said hi. When you're twelve you can stick with her on the first days of whatever treatment she's doing then," I promised. "I'll step aside and let you have a turn."

Tucker shook his head. "I won't be twelve for more than a year," he said.

"I know."

He just shook his head again. "I'd better go. They're loading the bus." He turned and walked away, Frankie at his side. I stared after him.

He knew something he wasn't telling me.

"Ready?" Annie grabbed her backpack and I grabbed mine. We headed to the coffee shop and walked in. No one we knew was there. I sighed with relief. It was nice to be anonymous sometimes.

It felt good to think that no one in the place knew we were on Planet Cancer. They all assumed we were on Planet Earth, just like them. One time last summer we went to a Seattle Mariners game. There were like thirty-six thousand people in the stadium. Since one in three people will get cancer in their lifetime, that meant there were twelve thousand people in that stadium that had cancer, or would get it, or had already had it. And that meant there were twenty-four thousand people like me who loved someone who had it. Most of them just didn't know it yet.

"Quinn!" Annie elbowed me.

I looked up. The barista was talking. Back to Planet Coffee. "Can I get something for you?"

"Um, yeah," I said. "How about a green Tazo tea with two raw sugars?"

Quinn's List of Drinks I Must Have While in Seattle, Before My Starbucks Card Runs Out of Credit

#1 Hazelnut White chocolate mocha with extra whipped cream

~~#2 Green Tazo tea with two packs of raw sugar~~

#3 Chantico Drinking Chocolate

~~#4 Double espresso. Straight up.~~

We sipped our drinks and talked about the shirt Annie was making and what to take to Leavenworth.

"I'd better get going." I looked at my watch. "My mom's treatment starts in half an hour, and I like to be there right when she's starting. She sometimes falls asleep after a bit."

Annie stood up with me. "I might walk up there with you."

"To the hill?" I asked, stunned.

She nodded and crumpled her cup, throwing it

into the garbage. I knew her mom was starting treatment today, too.

Wouldn't her mom be *so* excited to see her there, too? What a breakthrough. See? Something good was coming out of all of this mess. Annie was going to boldly walk up there, sit by her mom, and make a change for the better.

I almost skipped up the hill.

We walked into the treatment center—well, hospital, really.

I punched the elevator button. "Your mom is on the fifth floor, too," I said.

"I know," Annie answered.

The elevator doors opened and I got in. Annie hung back. "I'll wait for you down here."

Before I could protest the doors began to close. Other people were in the elevator, too, so it's not like I could have pushed the "door open" button and held them up, too.

The doors slammed shut. Annie turned her back on me.

I was so stunned that she wasn't going upstairs, I hardly knew what to think. I had just assumed she would be brave enough to do the whole deal, and I was kind of mad and ashamed that she wasn't. I mean, really. It's such a simple thing.

I knocked on the door of my mom's room. The nurse was still in there.

"It'll be just a minute," she reassured me. "I'm going to start your mom's medication."

"I'll wait outside," I said. It made me sick to see them hooking up the meds pump to the tube coming out of my mom's scarred, flat chest.

"It'll just take a second; it's a simple procedure," the nurse continued. "You can come on in if you'd like."

"No thanks," I said. I guess if you were a nurse it was a simple procedure since you'd done it a thousand times. But it was my mom. It gave me the willies to think about it.

I stood outside and watched them wheel a cart into Mercy Meyer's room. I thought about Annie.

I guess I hadn't felt good about visiting my mom when she was first going through chemo. I guess that's the other reason Dana always went, and inside I had been glad. Even after I had gone a few times, I still felt queasy. Like with seeing my mom's scars.

I'm sorry I thought that about Annie, God. I was being totally self-righteous. I leaned up against the hospital wall, watching the doctors and nurses rush around. I heard someone vomit in a room down the hall. It smelled like barf even where I was. I swallowed back the bile. Hearing someone vomit makes me want to vomit. It's like yawning. If someone else does it, it triggers the same reaction in everyone else.

But I'm trying everything I can to make Annie change, to get her to do things I think will make them happy. If that's not what I'm supposed to do, then tell me what I am supposed to do.

The nurse came out of my mom's room. "She's ready now," she said and winked at me.

I went in and sat by Mom. "How are you feeling?" I asked. Her skin looked kind of yellow, and it hadn't before.

She shook her head. "This treatment makes me more tired and sick than I thought it would," she said. "I don't think I can talk too much, because the medicine they give me to make the nausea go away makes me sleepy."

"Can I read to you?" I asked.

She smiled and nodded. "Yes."

I opened up *The Return of the King*. Since I'd read the books before, I sometimes read them all again in bits and pieces. Days like this I wished the King would return soon, even if that meant I would never get married and have kids of my own. Which I really wanted to do.

An hour later Mom was fast asleep. I pulled the conversation hearts out of her bag. I left two this time: *1 I Luv* and *U R Kind*. Then I shrugged off my worries and went downstairs.

When I got to the lobby, I didn't see Annie at first. I walked down a side hall and then I saw her, hanging outside the rest room door.

"Do you need to use it before we go home?" I asked.

She shook her head. "Already did."

"I saw your mom's room," I said. I wasn't trying to make her feel bad. I just wanted her to know that I had been thinking about her.

She nodded and looked across the hall. "Is that where you go on Sundays?"

The small room marked "Sanctuary" was there.

I nodded. "Yes."

Annie walked over. I was shocked when she stood outside with her hand on the door. "Do you have time to go in?"

"Oh yeah, sure," I said.

We walked into the room. The walls were lined with pale blue tiles that grew lighter as they got closer to the ceiling—on their way to heaven. Bamboo chairs waited timelessly in small rows in a semicircular pattern. There were no dark woods, no dark colors. Everything oozed the feeling of lightness. Except that the True Light, Jesus, had to share the wall with other faiths. There was a small stained-glass window in the shape of a cross but also banners with other faiths on them hanging on the wall. At first that had made me sad, but then I remembered that last year in youth group we'd learned a passage in the Bible that said something about wherever a Christian went she brought the fragrance of Christ into that place. I figured that when I was in here I brought Christ in with me.

I fingered my cross necklace while Annie looked through the books in the back of the room. She opened a Bible and paged through it. The she closed it and put it back on the shelf.

I sat in one of the chairs, quietly, waiting for her. A soft waterfall trickled and drizzled against some smooth stones in the fountain in one corner. I closed my eyes and felt my shoulder muscles uncoil. A citrus lavender scent arose from somewhere—like the smell when my mom grated lemon peel for cheesecake, mixed with the smell of the powder sachets tucked in her pajama drawer. It soothed me.

Annie sat down next to me. "What's that?" She pointed to a big bowl in the center of the room.

"The blessings bowl," I said.

She looked at me funny.

"I never heard of one before, either," I said. "The bowl is filled with nice thoughts on pieces of paper. I suppose they're like a fortune in a fortune cookie. If you want to make something good out of it, like advice, you can."

She sat there for a minute. "I'm going to get one."

"Okay," I said. I was going to tell her we could take one of those Bibles off the shelf if she wanted to read the Word and get a real blessing, but something stopped me and held me in my seat. I think it was God.

Annie went forward and I sat still. *What else can I do?*

I glanced at the books in the bookshelf again. One word caught my eye among the hundreds of titles with their many words.

Pray.

I knew God was talking to me. I didn't close my eyes because I didn't need to.

Thank you, Lord, for talking to me. I don't know why I hear your voice so much more strongly now than I ever did before. I feel your hand on my shoulder, your spirit in my heart. Heal my mom upstairs, God. Make this treatment work for her and help her to see me drive and grow up—and Tucker, too.

I looked at Annie drawing a slip of pink paper from the blessing bowl. I knew she'd pick pink. I bet God did, too. Were all the pink messages the same, all for Annie, to make sure she'd pick the one He wanted her to read? Or would He just guide her hand to the one He wanted her to have? Could God use that piece of paper even if a Christian person didn't write the message?

Help Annie, too. I don't know what to pray for her except for her to feel your love like I feel your love.

God doesn't always answer me right away, but ever since my mom got cancer, I feel like my ears hear softer whispers.

The whole passage came back to me right then.

Now wherever we go he uses us to tell others about the Lord and to spread the Good News like a sweet perfume. Our lives are a fragrance presented by Christ to God. But this fragrance is perceived differently by those being saved and by those perishing. To those who are perishing we are a fearful smell of death and doom. But to those who are being saved we are a life-giving perfume.

Be perfume.

I whispered back. "I remember it now."

Just then Annie came back with the pink slip of paper, which she folded and slipped into her pocket.

"I'm going to email Sun-Hea," she said, more firmly than I'd ever heard her speak. "It's time that we talked, sister to sister."

I really wanted to know what that blessing slip had said, but I didn't want to pry.

As we left the Sanctuary, I turned around. The room was growing darker as evening approached, but a ray of light came directly through the stained-glass cross, illuminating the whole room and casting a cross shadow across the other religions' banners on the opposite walls.

Hi, Jesus. He speaks to me in a lot of different ways, and if I pay attention I recognize most of them. His sheep know His voice.

Things I Will Pray for Annie

#1 That she will find Jesus waiting for her

#2 That she will meet Sun-Hea

#3 That she will make peace with her mom having cancer

#4 That her parents will fall in love again

CHAPTER SIX

My house was still warm when we arrived, of course, because Daddy had left only a few hours before to drive to Seattle. Dana had driven to Seattle to pick us up and bring us to Leavenworth. She and her husband were staying at our home this weekend so CJ could spend some time with Tucker and so we'd have chaperones and rides. And so Tucker and I could be in our own beds, for once. I wished Velveeta could have been there, too, but since we'd be away from the house much of the weekend, it was best for her to stay at the Maxwells'. My little hermit crab, too.

Annie explored my room. "This is so cool. I love how you have it decorated."

I looked around my room: a fake gold ring from *The Lord of the Rings* on my dresser, a poster of Orlando Bloom (*have* to take that *down*), and a full set of armor that someone had donated to Goodwill once and we bought. I like history, as long as it's in fiction and not in school.

"What does your room look like?" I asked.

"Lots of stuff I sewed by myself. The bedspreads and the curtains and fringes. It's kind of psychedelic," she said. "Neon colors. A huge cutout of a Volkswagen Bug on the wall with a picture of me pasted in the driver's seat. That's the kind of car I want when I start driving."

"When will you be fifteen?" I asked.

"In September. But in Kansas we can get an instruction permit at fourteen. I'm going to do that right when I get home. My parents promised."

"Get out! You can start driving *now*?"

"In a few weeks. February sixteenth, if I have my way." Annie's eyes twinkled. The day after she got home.

It was so unfair. She'd be driving before me. Just like the rest of my friends.

Tucker and CJ were playing Ping-Pong in the rec room downstairs. When they came up for dinner, Tucker had worked up a sweat and wore the first full smile I'd seen him wear all week.

We forked down pot roast and potatoes that someone from church had delivered. Then we went back upstairs to get ready.

"It's nice of your church to bring all of this over," Annie said.

I nodded. I guess I kind of took it for granted sometimes, how nice everyone had been to us. I hadn't ever thought about what all this would have been like without my church.

"What are you going to wear?"

"Your chocolate brown sweater, some jeans that are a little faded in front, and the button-up boots," I answered. "I have some brown crystal earrings that hang like teardrops. How about you?"

"I don't know. I was waiting to see what you chose so I could fit in." Annie twisted a hair ribbon around her fingers till they were striped with red. "How about my powder pink sweater and some jeans and my Etnies?"

"Cool. And pull your hair back so we can see your pink pearl earrings. They're really pretty."

Annie blushed. She looked so much better here, somehow, than in Seattle. Maybe because we actually had *sun*!

"Ready, girls?" Dana called upstairs. I put one more pat of powder on my face and some Sephora lipgloss— the only makeup I was allowed to wear till I was fifteen.

Dana tried to make small talk in the car. She really was a good friend to my mom. She went the long way and avoided Mountain View Road.

I knew why she did that. The cemetery was there.

One time last summer she was driving Tucker and me to swimming lessons, right after my mom found out "It" was back. We drove past Mountain View Road, and the sight of the cemetery made me burst out crying. Dana took me home instead of to swimming lessons.

I was glad Dana went the long way this time.

Ten minutes later we pulled up in front of church, and Annie and I stepped out of the car. "Call me when you want to come home, okay?" Dana said.

"Thank you," I said. "I hope I can help you back someday."

"You can help both your mom and me tomorrow," she said, smiling. I gulped some air. I'd temporarily forgotten about my part tomorrow.

Annie looked at me quizzically.

"I'll tell you later," I whispered. Just then we were attacked. By a Pack of Cats.

"QUIIIIIINN!" the voices came screaming across the sidewalk, and all of my friends, led, of course, by the fabulous Holly, came racing across to hug me. I was so proud of them. They hugged Annie right in, too, made us both the jelly center in their doughnut.

"You must be Annie," Holly said. "Quinn told us that she was bringing a friend."

Annie smiled at me, and I knew she felt right away that it was going to be okay.

Inside the Dungeon everyone was already hanging out playing foosball and pinball, and the music was *loud*. We went over to one of the tables and sat down. Each table had a huge bowl of Moose Munch in the middle of it.

"Moose Munch," Holly said. "It's our national symbol."

We all rolled our eyes. "Okay, not national. But it *is* the signature of our youth group. Everyone eats it. We bring it to every retreat and camp."

"It's popcorn with chocolate drizzled on it," I whispered to Annie. "You don't have to eat it if you don't want. Kind of like candy, you know."

Annie grabbed a handful and made sure everyone could see her eat it. They all smiled at her. I knew she wanted to belong.

From the back of the room, I watched the door. I

talked with everyone, of course, but I was distracted, I admit. I rubbed my boot over the nubby carpet and picked at the arm of the couch I'd moved to. I kept looking up at the metal-framed door.

"Whatcha watching?" Holly teased me. "People doing Dance Dance Revolution?"

"Ha-ha," I said. I blushed. They all knew. Anyway, what were friends for?

When the door opened and he walked in with his group of friends, I felt a little jump inside, like when you touch the carpet and get a static shock. Adam smiled and waved over in my direction. I was *not* going to get up and walk over to him. I would wait and see if he came over to me.

He didn't rush, but he did make his way back. He came and sat down next to me, and the Pack of Cats grabbed Annie and skittered over to the pinball machines. They melted into the background, like good friends would, and Adam and I sat munching Munch.

"So how ya doin'?"

"Okay," I said. "My friend Annie came with me."

"I saw her," he said, but his look told me all I wanted to know about dark-haired sophisticated girls versus pretty blondes. "I'm glad you're back. Do you want to play pool for a while?"

We did and had a great time, although I tried hard not to get sweaty. Not exactly the look I was after. Then we sat down and talked about the youth part of the Valentine's party.

"I think it's all together," he said. "Everything except the flower sale, which is going to be a big fund-raiser for our mission trip this summer. We have the florist arranged—but you want to make up the individual price tags and organize making the flower arrangements when you come back, right?"

I nodded. "Yeah, it's really important to me that I get to do at least one important part. I'll be back in enough time. Plenty of time."

Adam stepped closer to me, and suddenly I found it kind of hard to breathe. I think he was growing a mustache. Really! I hadn't noticed it before, but he was, a little. I think he was taller than when I left a few weeks ago, too. Also, I never noticed that green was a really, really good color on him. It made his eyes look more green than blue. I hoped he'd wear green to the Valentine's party. Was there some way to tell him that without sounding too girlfriendy? Which we really were not. Exactly. Officially. You know.

"I told Marcie and Michelle that you'd be back in time. Marcie thought if you needed to give it up, Michelle could take over."

Who was Michelle?

Adam must have seen the look on my face. "Michelle is a new girl. She was in youth group over

Christmas, but maybe you didn't meet her."

Uh, no.

"Anyway, she signed up to help with the Valentine's party. I don't know if she'll be here tonight or not."

"Oh, what does she look like?" I tried to sound casual. "I just wondered if maybe that would help me remember her."

"Dark hair. Like yours. Kind of taller."

Drat.

"Well, I'd really like to handle the flower arranging," I said. "It was totally important to my mom that we be with her in Seattle, but I'll be back in time to do the flowers. Because it's important to me to stay a part of this, too, when the rest of my life is so, ah, unpredictable."

Adam smiled for me. I think it was only for me, and I felt reassured for the moment. "I told you I wouldn't let anyone take your green beanbag," he said. We headed over to the corner, and I sat down on *my* beanbag. Holly and the others came over, and Adam's friends did, too, and we played Cranium till we were sick of Moose Munch and our heads pounded with music and our hearts were full of fun. Before we left, Holly handed me a piece of paper. I opened it up.

My name was on top, and then there was a list of each day for the next few weeks till I would come home. Someone's name was next to each day to pray for *me*!

"The guys' names were my idea," Adam said. "Holly told me her idea, and I knew you needed more names because it's, like, over three weeks till you're back."

"Thanks, guys." I hugged as many as I could reach. Annie hung back.

"I knew people were praying for your mom, because my mom is on that list," Holly said. "I thought it would be good for you, too."

I wiped my eyes. I couldn't help it. The veins of sorrow and worry and fear ran so close to my skin that it took only a tiny scratch to bring the blood to the surface. I noticed that Annie had dropped back, and I grabbed her hand and brought her in the middle of the group again.

On the way out Annie stopped at a table that had books and Bibles and stuff on it. She rubbed her hand over one of the Bibles. Of course! This is why the Lord had held me back at the Sanctuary. She was going to take one here. "Would you like one?" I asked her. "They're free giveaways."

She took her hand off of the Bible and shook her head. "No thanks." Then she picked up one of the pretty golden suncatchers. We girls had each gotten one last year at camp. They hung in our bedroom windows to catch the sun as it came into our rooms. I had brought mine to Seattle with me, so Annie hadn't seen it in my room here.

"Those are free, too," I said. "We all have one; if you want one you can be one of us!"

Annie smiled. "I'd like that." She put one into her deep winter coat pocket.

We all walked outside together and hung out till the parents—and Dana—came to pick us up.

Later that night Annie and I lay awake chatting. I had a trundle bed, so I slept in my bed and Annie on the one that pulled out. We both had fuzzy toe socks on—a funny coincidence. Mine had Kermit the Frog and hers had a monkey.

"Thanks for inviting me," Annie said.

"Did you have a good time?"

"Totally," she said, and I could tell she meant it. "You have great friends."

"Yeah, and they all love God," I said. Annie looked funny then, and I felt so *stupid* because I remembered she wasn't a Christian. *Button the gums,* I thought.

"So where are we going tomorrow?" Annie asked.

"To the Ribbons in the Snow thing for a while," I answered. "I have to open with the prayer. And then we can go out for German food. Didn't you say you were German? We have a lot of cool German restaurants in town. You'll love it."

"Ribbons in the Snow?"

"Oh, did I forget to tell you? It's a cross-country skiing fund-raiser for breast cancer that my mom started in town last year. My mom felt really sad that she had to have treatment during the event tomorrow—especially since she had set the whole thing up—so her friend Debbie arranged for me to say the opening prayer! Yikes!"

"Tomorrow?" Annie asked.

"Yeah, I know. I hope I don't blow it. I mean, in front of all those people. For my mom."

Annie fell back against her bed and said nothing for a minute as the air sighed out of her pillow. "Would it be okay if I stayed here with Tucker?"

I propped up on my elbows. "Tucker is coming. We're going to cross-country ski some of the course." *Oh, I get it.* "You don't have to ski, no problem. I didn't even ask if you skied."

"I ski," Annie said. "I'm just not into going to cancer things. I told you, this is a little incident in our lives, and then we're going back home. It's just not something I feel like breathing and eating all the time like you people." She looked over. "I hope that doesn't hurt your feelings."

Not breathing it all the time? A little incident? She should be ready to deal with it.

I opened my mouth to tell her so, and then I closed it again. All of a sudden a picture of Dana taking the long way to avoid what I couldn't face came into my mind.

It's not the same, Lord, I said in my heart. *I mean, really.*

I heard nothing back.

"No problem, we'll just come back here and get you afterward. You can sit in my room and read, as long as it's okay with your parents."

Annie nodded and smiled. "Thanks. I'll work on sewing my head wraps."

It just didn't seem right to point out that they were for cancer. I got it. Maybe she would on her own.

We chatted that night about youth group and my friends. And Adam.

"He's cute," Annie said. "Does he have a brother I might be interested in?" she teased.

"Mm-hmm," I said. "He's eight years old."

Annie threw a pillow at me and we chatted some more before reading. I pulled an old devotional off of my shelf. I kind of missed reading the Bible. I didn't make much time for that in Seattle, but being in church at home again had reminded me.

The next morning Annie braided my hair, and I pulled my Norwegian knit ski cap over it. "Are you sure I won't have hat hair when I take the hat off?"

"I'm sure," she said. "That's why I did the side braids."

Okay. I have to admit, it looked good. Sophisticated.

I wondered how long Michelle's hair was. Hmph.

Tucker and I grabbed our skis and boots and poles and headed toward the car. Dana was ready. I tucked my mittens into my pocket so my hands wouldn't sweat too much before I got there. They were already damp. I had never prayed in front of a hundred people.

"Ready?" Dana asked me.

I nodded.

"You're not only representing God, you're representing your mom, too."

Thanks, Dana. A little stress with my Cheerios this morning.

We pulled into the open fields next to Johnson's Woods, where the event was going to start. A fire was roaring in the pit, and there were urns of hot chocolate at a table loaded with apple strudel.

I took a strip of strudel and bit into it. The pastry melted onto my tongue like morning snowflakes, the apples polka-dotted with cinnamon-butter and enfolded into the pastry like a kid in Grandma's arms. Yum. I took another slice and yanked Tucker's hands off of the tray. He'd already had three slices.

"The podium is over here," Dana said.

I walked up to it and stood back while everyone else got organized. Suddenly I was overcome by sadness. Everyone here had been touched by cancer in some way—either they'd had it or someone they loved did.

Most people with breast cancer survive. Some do not. Most are cured. Some are terminal.

My mom was terminal.

My mom was terminal.

I forced myself to think the thought for the first time, really, getting my heart around what that meant.

Even if this treatment was successful and it kept the cancer away from her brain for a few years, my mom would not be at my wedding. My mom would not be able to help me when my first baby had a fever. My mom might not see my high school graduation.

My eyes blurred with tears, and the whole scene looked like a sad watercolor. Tucker saw my face.

"Go ahead," he said. "You can do it."

If anyone else had said that, I would have hit them with an ice ball. But Tucker knew.

If the treatment worked, my mom *would* have a few more years to be able to see me drive. To talk to me after my first kiss. To take me shopping and go swimming again. That's what this was all about, right?

I felt God's presence settle on me like the flakes still falling from the sky. They melted away. He did not. He stayed.

I will never leave you or forsake you. Nothing will separate you—or your mom—from my love.

My mom would want me to do it.

"Thank you for having me," I stepped up and said, voice warbling. "My mom wishes she were here, but she can't be. Please pray with me.

"Lord, thank you for bringing all of these people here today, though I'm sorry for the reason they needed to come. Please help us enjoy your great outdoors and everything you created. Don't let anyone get injured today, Lord. They're all as old as my mom!"

I heard a ripple of laughter.

"Let us see you, Lord. Please heal the sick, Jesus. Every one. Amen."

I wobbled down and Dana brought me a cup of hot chocolate. I was done.

We skied till we were sore, but we raised a lot of money, money that would go to research to help women like my mom. Women like Mercy Meyer.

I walked into the house just before dinnertime.

"How did it go?" Annie asked.

"Fine," I said. "Do you want to go out for dinner?"

She nodded. Before we got ready, I saw her set her book back into her suitcase. It was her math book. Saving her place was the thin strip of paper she'd withdrawn from the blessings bowl last Monday.

It must be really important to her if she kept it with her every day.

She leaned over and whispered in my ear. "I wrote an email to Sun-Hea before I left. I found her email address in my dad's stuff. I told her to plan to come."

She wrapped her purse strings around her fingers and back again, leaving indentations and welts. "I haven't told my parents yet."

"I'll pray for you," I said.

"I knew you would." She smiled.

"I think you're doing great with all this stuff with your sister," I said. "In the middle of your mom's sickness and all."

She looked at me, surprised, and said nothing at all. I think she was dumbfounded.

We ate at Yodel House and tapped our foot to the music and sang songs from *The Sound of Music*. It was fun. Annie bought two extra huge pretzels to wrap up and bring back for her dad. Her mom's mouth was too broken out in sores to eat anything that wasn't mush.

I should put G Kitty on the job. She could mush anything in the Veggo.

The next morning we went to church before we left to go back to Seattle. I met Michelle.

I saw her before she saw me—I had the advantage of knowing that she was Marcie's friend and that she had dark hair. She was pretty. *Drat.*

Holly sat next to us, of course, and at the end of Sunday school she handed an envelope to Annie.

"Thanks," Annie said.

"You can open it in the car on the way back to Seattle," Holly said. Then she hugged her. "Nice to meet you!"

I wondered what was in there. I smiled. If I knew Holly, it was something nice. Encouraging. Kind. Annie would tell me, sooner or later. I hoped.

Annie hugged her back. My whole group hugged me, too, because we were on our way back to Seattle right after church. I hoped my dad would wait for us to get there before he left, or I wouldn't get to see him all week.

Adam and his friends came over to say good-bye, too. They each gave me a hug, but I think Adam's was extra tight. It was, I know it was.

"See you in three weeks, Q," he said. "I'll email."

I know he was skiing a lot and didn't have as much time to email. Plus, I just don't think guys do that as much as we girls do. So I was glad he said it.

"Me too," I promised. His eyes twinkled. Just for me, I hoped.

When I turned around, Marcie and Michelle had gone.

Tucker, Annie, and I sat in the backseat as Dana headed the car out toward the highway away from home, back to Planet Cancer. The three of us felt sick.

Tucker tried really hard not to cry, but I could see him struggling.

"Want me to build a card house with you when we get back?" I asked.

"I told you I'm never doing them again."

"I bought something for you," I said.

He looked uninterested. "Thanks," he said.

I whipped out the deck of cards and the book of card tricks. "If you work hard, you could probably have four card tricks to wow CJ and all of your friends with at the Valentine's party when we get home," I said. "Tricks they never heard of and won't be able to figure out."

He perked up. "Let me see that." He opened the book. "The directions are kind of hard to understand. Will you help me?"

I ruffled his hair. Tucker always understood directions. He was the ultimate straight-A nerd. He was tired, too. "Of course I'll help you, Lemonhead," I said.

He stuck his tongue out at me, and I knew it would be okay.

We started looking through the book for some really stunning tricks that his friends would never be able to duplicate. Out of the corner of my eye, I saw Annie open up her envelope from Holly and read the paper before folding it back up and sticking it into her purse. Her eyes welled with tears.

I know it was for her, but it was *my* best friend who had written it. I was dying to know what was in there.

"Hey," Tucker said. "What about this one?"

Four Tricks to Teach Tucker
Before Valentine's Day

#1 All the Aces
#2 Hotel and Motel
#3 Order, Please
#4 Vanishing Card

CHAPTER SEVEN

When we got back to Anderson House, my dad had already left. My mom looked so pretty, though. It was the first time I'd seen her put on a real pair of jeans and a sweater in a long time, instead of the sweats she usually wore to the hospital and for lounging around the apartment.

"Dad and I went shopping yesterday," she said. "He left a present for you."

I could already see Tucker tearing into a gift-wrapped box in the living room and then dancing and whooping as he pulled out the latest Xbox game. Dad had brought his Xbox down this weekend, too. "For our weekend warrior sessions," Tucker said.

"Aren't you going to open your gift?" Mom said. She handed a small box to me. It was wrapped in orange and silver paper and looked like an expensive creamsicle.

I unwound the ribbon and let it fall softly to the floor. I opened the box. It read, "Demeter Tiger Lily Pick-Me-Up Cologne Spray."

"Oh," I sighed. "Real perfume. Not Love's Baby Soft anymore."

Mom nodded. "And it's Tiger Lily."

"I noticed," I said. My dad's nickname for me. I sprayed some on the inside of my wrist, and a single note of flower laced the air.

"Sweet and sassy just like you." Mom ruffled my hair.

That night after dinner, I took a shower. As I lathered up my hair, I decided to buy some of that brunette shine shampoo I'd seen. I bet Michelle didn't use that. My hair would be totally shiny by Valentine's Day.

I threw on my Kermit pj's and padded into our room. As soon as I entered the room, Tucker turned his back to me. I ran up to him and reached around him.

"You little snoop!" I said. "That is *my* journal and those are *my* lists."

"They are not," he said. "They're Mom's."

"How dare you?" I grabbed the lists from his hands. "Mom gave them to *me*. And how do you know they're Mom's, anyway?"

"I saw the handwriting," Tucker said, backing away from me like a mouse from a cat. "But I didn't read them."

He skeddadled away from me and into Mom's room to say good-night. I slammed the door behind him and sat on the bed.

God, I want my real life back. I want to be in my own room in Leavenworth, without my prying brother, in a house with my dad and mom. I put the lists between two pairs of my underwear in my drawer. I knew he wouldn't find them there.

By the next morning I had cooled off. I knew my mom would feel the vibe if we were fighting, and besides, if he had read any of the last list he'd be moping around. He wasn't. He was amazingly chipper. More chipper, in fact, than I had seen him for a long time.

We walked down the hall to school. "What's up with the wide smiles?" I asked him.

"Oh, nothing. Must be all that nine-grain cereal," he said.

"Ha-ha," I said. "Tell me the truth."

He looked at me seriously. "I will," he said. "After school. If you take me to get a coffee before you go up the hill for Mom's treatment."

"Blackmail!" I said.

He nodded and whistled. "Yep." Then he turned down the hallway to the primary classroom. I smiled in spite of myself. It was good to see the old pesky Lemonhead back again.

"I'm going up the hill after school," I said to Annie during study hall. Annie turned from Ben for a minute and smiled at me.

"I'll be working on your shirt," she said. "Call me later." Then she turned back to Ben, whose face lit up as she focused on him again.

Tucker and I walked to Starbucks, and I told him he could order for both of us.

"Oh yeah. Two Chantico Drinking Chocolates," he told the barista. "With two cookies."

Quinn's List of Drinks I Must Have While in Seattle, Before My Starbucks Card Runs Out of Credit

#1 Hazelnut white chocolate mocha with extra whipped cream

#2 Green Tazo tea with two packs of raw sugar

#3 Chantico Drinking Chocolate

#4 Double espresso. Straight up.

"So what's up?" I asked him. I was trying not to be grumpy or look flinty-eyed at the people who had stolen the soft chairs.

"I lied to you." He took a long drink and licked the chocolate from his lips. "I'm sorry."

"What do you *mean* you lied to me?"

"I read the lists yesterday. Well, not all of them. But the one that Mom wrote where she said what she wanted to do before she died. Not all of it. Most of it."

"What did you see?"

"I think she's done everything on there except

dance the Hustle and fly a plane. I figured you could dance the Hustle with her, since I don't dance and neither does Dad. And I can help her fly the plane."

I didn't bother to tell him I'd already asked Dad about the Hustle.

"What do you mean you can help her fly the plane?"

He unfolded a wad of paper from his pocket and handed it to me.

" 'Making Memories,' " I read aloud. " 'Making dreams come true for cancer patients and their families.'" I scanned the rest of it and looked up at Tucker.

"The patients only have to *have* cancer," I said. "They don't have to be dying right away. Right?"

Tucker grew quiet. He unfolded another piece of paper from his pocket. "Since you shared your journal and lists with me—"

"Against my will," I said.

"—I'm going to show you this."

I took the second paper from him. It was a printout from the Cancer Center. "When the disease hits the brain, it often brings unsteadiness on the feet and loss of memory." I folded the paper up.

"Mom has been kind of clumsy," he said.

"I think she's just tired. The treatments make her tired. You'd probably stumble, too."

"She had a hard time remembering where she put

her purse and also what time G Kitty was supposed to be back last week."

"Treatment," I said firmly. I had seen the crocus growing when we'd been home last weekend. Spring was coming. I knew it was. That flower was a sign from God.

Tucker folded the paper up. "So what I wanted to ask is, is it okay if I email this Making Memories place to talk about flying a plane? And you can do the Hustle thing?"

I sat there, letting the last dribbles of chocolate linger on my tongue. If we did everything on Mom's list, would that be giving her permission to die? I mean, would we actually be making it easier for her to die because now she'd have done everything she said she wanted to? But what if the treatment wasn't quite as strong as we hoped? Would she be sad if she didn't do them all?

If Dad did the Hustle, and Tucker got the flight arranged, there would be nothing left for me to do.

"Go ahead and do it," I told him. "It's yours."

He kissed my cheek for the first time in a long time. I walked him back to the apartment before walking up the hill for the last treatment.

When I got to Mom's room, she was already asleep. The medication pump was hooked up. I sat there for a few minutes, and then her doctor stopped by the room.

"Quinn, right?" The doctor sat down by me.

"Yes," I said. I was seriously bummed that my mom was already asleep. I had talked too long with Tucker.

"We started a little early," she said. "I had another patient to get to, and your mom thought it would be okay. It's her last treatment, and then next week we'll test."

I nodded and said nothing.

"You've been a great help to her treatment," the doctor said. "Support is so necessary. The patients who get personal support often do better."

"Really?"

She nodded. "Really. You've been helping her to get healthy with everything you've done. Now we wait and see." She snapped her clipboard closed and nodded on her way out of the room.

Mom murmured a little. I saw her Bible by the side of her bed. She'd been reading Psalm 139. I read it out loud to her, quietly. Just in case my voice comforted her and she was in twilight sleep, from the medications, instead of real sleep. Maybe I could keep on helping.

I rubbed her hand lightly as I read. She used to do that for me when I was little to get me to sit and listen to her read longer without becoming restless.

"'Where can I go from your Spirit? Where can I flee from your presence? If I go up to the heavens, you are there; if I make my bed in the depths, you are there. If I rise on the wings of the dawn, if I settle on the far side of the sea, even there your hand will guide me, your right hand will hold me fast.'"

My mom stirred a little, and I let her settle before I continued. I pulled the blanket up to her chin, like she did for me and Tucker. I read some inside my head and then stopped rubbing her hand as I read the next sentence aloud. "'All the days ordained for me were written in your book before one of them came to be.'"

I left conversation hearts that said, *I Luv U* and *Come Home*.

The next day the volunteers threw a small party in the rec room on the first floor of Anderson House, our apartment building. One hundred people lived there, and about twenty volunteers were on hand to help. It was kind of fun. One of the other students had arranged it as a way to break up the winter blahs. I loved it. I'm a party girl at heart.

G Kitty brought spinach spanakopita. I brought cream hearts.

When I got downstairs, Annie and her dad were already deep in a card game with Tucker. Annie folded her cards and came to the side to talk with me.

"I heard back," she said quietly.

I raised my eyebrows in question.

"From Sun-Hea. She's coming." Annie grinned. "I have a sister and I'm going to meet her!"

"Great!" I said. "How did it happen?"

"Well, I've decided I need to be strong. Make decisions. I know that my mom was softening toward Sun-Hea, and I know my dad wanted to see her, too. I want a sister, and Sun-Hea wants to see me. It just seemed so simple. Simple, that is, unless you live in a family that never talks. So I talked. I emailed Sun-Hea and told her to plan on it."

"Do your parents know?" I asked.

Annie shook her head. "My mom's treatment will be finished soon, and then she'll be feeling great. I can tell her then."

"Okay." I hoped it happened that way for her. "I'm glad you are going to get to meet her," I said.

"Me too." She squeezed my hand.

"Can you girls help me?" G Kitty called from the serving area. There was music playing now and more people arriving.

We walked over. "My hands hurt and I can't get the lid off of this jar" Grandma Kitty said. I reached over and unscrewed it.

"You smell good," G Kitty commented.

"Yeah," Annie said. "I noticed that yesterday. Whenever you leave a place, you leave a tiny scent of that pretty perfume behind. It's lovely."

"Thanks," I said. "It's Tiger Lily." I felt proud, but I held myself back from asking Annie if she thought it was a sophisticated scent.

In one corner Tucker was showing Frankie the book of card tricks I'd given him. I whispered in his ear, "I thought you weren't going to show your friends your tricks? You know, dazzle and impress?"

He whispered back, "Frankie is okay. He's not going to be at the Valentine's party. He can dazzle and impress his friends at home, too."

I nodded my agreement and tousled his hair.

Later that night Tucker showed me the printouts he'd made of flight lessons at Boeing Field in Seattle.

"I emailed Making Memories," he said. "But I haven't heard back."

I nodded.

"You don't think that's going to make her die, do you?" he asked. "I mean, if we help her finish her list?"

"No," I answered.

"Do you think she knows something?" he asked. "Is

that why she wanted us to come to Seattle with her instead of staying at home with Dad?"

"I think Mom just didn't want to be alone with G Kitty and the couscous for dinner," I teased. "She needed us to protect her tastebuds."

Tucker giggled and went to get his pj's.

I went to find Kermit. And my journal to mark my progress.

I was helping my mom. The doctor had said so!

Quinn's New Year's Resolutions

#1 ~~Help mom stay healthy.~~

#2 Drive a car before any of my friends. I am not kidding. Otherwise I will ONCE AGAIN be last since all my friends will turn 15 before I do. I just want to be first, at one thing that is important, for once.

#3 Make an unhealthy meal that Grandma Kitty says tastes delicious.

#4 Get kissed by a boy. Not Tucker.

CHAPTER EIGHT

Hey.'' Annie caught up with me Wednesday after class. "I know you need to walk Tucker home, but I wondered if you could go somewhere with me afterward?"

"Sure," I said. "As long as Grandma Kitty says it's okay. Is your dad going to drive?"

Annie tucked her books into her backpack and tucked her blond waves behind her ears. "We can walk. I want to go back to the Sanctuary."

I stopped for a minute but then kept walking.

Cool! I think she was like a little bird that alighted on a safe branch but might fly away if startled off. I didn't want to spook her. "Sure," I said. "Any time."

We went home to eat, since neither of us had brought lunches that day, and for me to drop Tucker off, and then we met in the lobby. Mom wouldn't get home from treatment until later in the afternoon, so I felt okay about going with Annie.

As we walked up the hill, I noticed more crocuses peeking out. The hyacinths smelled like G Kitty's all natural, no additives floral perfume. "Spring is coming," I said. "Can you smell it?"

"No," Annie said. "I can smell the faint scent of Tiger Lily, though. It smells kind of . . ." She seemed to look for the right word.

"Sophisticated?" I offered teasingly.

She snapped her fingers. "That's it!" She laughed. I hadn't seen her so happy in a long time. I wondered if something was going on with her mom's treatment or if her mom was feeling good today. All of us, all of our moods, were driven by that.

"I'm glad we're going to the Sanctuary," I said. "I'm just kind of curious about why, if you don't mind telling me."

The wind blew strands of my hair into my face, and I pushed them back so I could look at her while we finished the rest of the climb.

"I got an email," she said. "Well, two."

"Cool! From Sun-Hea?"

"Mm-hmm. She uploaded a picture and said she doesn't have any other brothers or sisters, either, so she's really looking forward to meeting me."

"What if she emails your dad with the plans before you tell him?" I asked.

Annie stopped dead. "Oh. I hadn't thought of that. I guess I'd better tell him before she does. If she hasn't emailed him already." Her walk slowed down. I was sorry I had brought it up; it had been so nice to see her happy again.

"Tell me about the other email," I tried.

"Oh, that." She pulled a piece of paper out of her peach shirt pocket and let me read it. It was from Holly! *My* Holly!

I scanned it. They had all signed up to pray for Annie every day till Valentine's Day, since she was going home the day after, just like they had with me. This was why Holly had slipped Annie that note before we left Leavenworth. I looked over the list of names. Michelle—tall, dark Michelle—had signed up for Annie's list even though she hadn't appeared on my list.

Adam was on there, too. I was okay with that, though.

"I think it's so cool that your friends are going to

pray for me. So I wanted to try praying myself," Annie said.

We walked into the building and down the hall toward the Sanctuary.

Something about her last comment bugged me.

I held the door of the Sanctuary open for her, and she strode through. A small man was kneeling by a corner chair. A few minutes after we arrived, he got up and left.

Annie sat on one chair and I sat next to her. I looked at those banners on the walls that showed all kinds of different religions. Then I saw a small stained-glass window on the left wall. This one showed Jesus in the garden. I wanted to rush up and get Annie a Bible from the bookshelf to make sure she understood to whom she needed to pray, not just someone from any of these religions, which were not all the same. Only the Living God could help her.

I felt that hand of God holding me back, though. *Wait.* So I didn't move. Annie didn't go to the blessings bowl this time, but she did go up and write a prayer request in the prayer request book. So did I. Then I sat back down and prayed again my request.

Lord, thank you for this hospital.

Please let Mom's test results come back okay. With at least two, no, at least three years to live. And let Tucker's airplane ride come out okay and help Dad learn the Hus-

tle. God, I feel bad about my not doing anything special, but would you please make my mom okay with that and help her to see how much she means to me? Help Annie see you, Lord. Take her blindfold off so she can see you waiting for her.

I tried hard to remember what I had jotted down in my journal to pray for her. I took the folded stack of Mom's lists out of my journal and then paged through the notebook till I found the right one. Annie looked at me out of one open eye, pursed her lips in disapproval, and went back to praying.

What's up with that?

Annie had closed her eyes again and clasped her hands like I used to when I said my bedtime prayers.

Things I Will Pray for Annie

#1 That she will find Jesus waiting for her

#2 That she will meet Sun-Hea

#3 That she will make peace with her mom having cancer

#4 That her parents will fall in love again

Number two I could cross off, even though she was going to have to talk with her dad pronto. What if he already knew?

Number one I had just prayed for.

Also, Jesus, help her to make peace with her mom hav-

ing cancer. Help her mom and dad to fall in love again. Thank you for giving me a friend on Planet Cancer. I wish I could help her more. I know, I know, Mom says praying is helping.

In a hurry, I stuffed Mom's lists back into my journal, shoved the notebook into the pocket of my backpack, and looked at Annie. She was staring at me.

"Your eyes were open," she said as we exited the Sanctuary.

"Yeah, that's okay," I said. "I close them if I need to concentrate, but you don't have to close your eyes to pray."

"Oh," she said, shrugging her shoulders into her sweater.

Suddenly I understood. "You don't have to be in a church or the Sanctuary to pray, either. You can pray wherever you are, whenever you want. God is with us, listening, everywhere."

Annie's face lit up. "Cool." She opened her backpack and took the pink slip of paper out of it, the one from the blessings bowl from last time. She handed it to me.

"You sure you want me to read it?"

She nodded and I opened the paper and read, "Be strong. Make decisions."

I folded it up and handed it back. "What do you think that means?"

We were almost home now. She stared at me, open-mouthed. "I am not totally powerless. I can do things. Like email Sun-Hea. Like, ah, think about God and pray for my mom. Maybe even throw a party. With your help."

Right out of the blue that came, like a UFO. Now it was *my* turn to stop dead. "Throw a party? My help? What kind of party?"

"A Valentine's party."

My hands got cold. "I'd like to help," I said. "But I'm not going to be here for Valentine's Day."

"I know," she said. She buzzed the door to Anderson House and the watchman let us in. "I don't expect you to. But I just got this great idea when we were at your house in Leavenworth last weekend." She pointed toward the rec room. "Do you have a minute to sit in there with me?"

I was intrigued. Of course I had a minute!

We walked into the huge rec room. It took up almost the entire lower floor of the apartment building. We'd had our little party there yesterday and used up only a quarter of the space. The polished wooden floor warmed the room, and lots of low windows let in great gulps of light. The furniture—all donated—was leather and lovely. We sat down in two of the cushy chairs and grabbed bottled water, stocked in the room's fridge.

"Well, my mom's favorite holiday is Valentine's Day.

I had been thinking that I could make a few decorations for our apartment, since we'll still be here, but then the other day a couple of ideas started gelling."

I unscrewed my water cap and motioned for her to continue.

"So when we were at your house and I heard more about the Valentine's party, I kept thinking, what a great idea. But of course we couldn't make it to Leavenworth and then back here in time for our plane early the next day. And my parents might feel awkward at your church. And my mom's immune system will still be weak from chemo."

"So you thought about here?" I asked.

"Not until last night, when we had everyone down here for the party. Then I thought—hey, why not? Why not a Valentine's party for everyone here? They know not to invite anyone sick."

I finished my water. "I think it's a great idea. What do you want me to do?"

"Plan it," Annie said. "That is, if you don't mind putting in all that work on a party you won't even get to go to."

Hmm. It probably was going to be a lot of work. But then I thought of my mom, who had worked so hard on Ribbons in the Snow, and what she had said. That the truest test of success was if the things you set in motion thrive even if you aren't there to supervise it all.

"Why don't you want to plan it?" I asked.

Annie giggled. "Last time I planned an event, the only thing I could come up with was wacky banana games." Her smile dimmed a little. "Really. I worked up all the courage to suggest it and they froze me out of the committee."

Ooh, what snobs. I didn't say it in case they were her friends.

"Anyway, I want it to be really good, and I know you know what you're doing from your own party. Will you do it?"

I toyed with her. "Well, ah, um, hmm . . ."

"I'll see if my dad will take us to the craft store after school tomorrow. The one we bought your material at. Plus, if you're helping with the party, I'll be sure to have time to finish your shirt before *your* party," she teased.

Okay, two could play at that game. I was glad to see her spunk back.

Her eyes twinkled. She knew I was going to say yes.

"Only," I said, "if you ask Ben to help us. You have to ask him tomorrow."

"Ben?" She seemed taken aback. "I thought you liked Adam. At home."

"I do," I said. "But *you* want Ben there, don't you?"

She punched my arm. I punched hers back.

We were on.

⚊

The next day after school I searched the Web for party ideas. I came across a site that listed—I am not kidding—wacky banana games.

Annie came up behind me and I clicked off the screen. "I did it," she said.

"You did what?"

"I asked Ben to help. He thought it was a great idea."

I caught a glimpse of Ben, tall and lanky and spinning a basketball on his fingertips as he chatted with another guy in our class. I waved at him and he waved back.

I grinned. "Of course it's a great idea. I'm looking for stuff we can buy right now."

"I checked with the volunteer committee this morning, like you suggested. They said yes and gave me a budget to work with," Annie said. "My dad said he'd take us shopping tonight. He'll pay for everything and submit the receipt to the volunteers. That fabric store we went to had a huge craft and party section. Would that be okay?"

I nodded. "Except for the food. We'll have to ask the volunteer staff to help us with that later."

Annie beamed. "My dad was really glad to help. This is going to mean *so* much to my mom. She's never had a Valentine's party, even though it's her favorite holiday. I don't actually think anyone has ever thrown her any kind of party."

"How are your parents doing these days?" I asked

"Better. My mom's been happier lately, and Dad's happier, too. I think he enjoyed playing basketball with your dad last weekend."

What? She must have seen the look on my face.

"Yeah, I guess they went to play basketball last Saturday while my mom went with your mom to a seminar on the hill about something. My mom didn't tell me what the seminar was about. No surprise there."

Well, it *was* a surprise to me. My mom told me everything about her treatment. Or so I thought.

"Anyway," Annie said, "be ready at seven. Okay?"

I nodded. She left and I went back to surfing. I bookmarked the page I'd been hiding from her and went back to decorations and recipes.

Hey now. One caught my eye. "Put some 'heart' in

your party. Double Heart Attack Fettuccine Carbonara."

I read the recipe. Tons of cream. Lots of noodles. Heart clogging cheese. *Bacon!* I could barely contain myself. I wondered if Annie's dad would be willing to stop at Safeway on the way home from the craft store.

I stopped by the desk at Fitzschool on my way home and arranged to have a volunteer call me later in the weekend to see how she could help us. Our party was underway!

When I got home I checked my email, even though I'd just checked it at school. My heart stopped. An email from Adam!

"Tomorrow is my day to pray for you, Q," he wrote. *"But I've been praying every day. I hope your mom will come through okay. God is faithful. Is there anything else I can do?"*

I thought for a minute. Okay.

Quinn's List of Things Adam Can Do

#1 Wear a green shirt to the Valentine's party.

#2 Stay far away from Michelle. Like the plague. Like she's invisible.

#3 Help me complete something on my list.

#4 Send me the email address of the florist for the party so I can finish planning the flower sale for the dance.

I giggled at number three. I mean, which one could he help me with? Ha-ha.

I didn't write numbers one, two, and three on my list. I kept them in my heart, though.

I wrote back to Adam.

Hey there,
  Thanks for emailing me. It always cheers me up to hear about what's going on at home. Send more news!

Then I told him about our Valentine's party here.

I'm going to plan it, but then Annie will take over. Speaking of that, can you help me with something? Can you send me the email address of the florist so I can get that going? Say hi to everyone for me. I'll be home soon. Green beanbag. Mine.
                    Q

After supper I went into my room to change. Jean skirt. Brown sweater. Button-up boots.

G Kitty dozed on the living room chair, and my mom dozed in her bedroom. That was one of the real bummers about cancer treatments. My mom was always asleep. Before cancer, I am not kidding you, my mom was a dynamo. After chemo and before "It" came back, she was like Speedy Gonzales.

I went into the bathroom to fix my hair. Forty-five minutes till we left. I tossed my brush under the sink and put in some new earrings. I tried on some of G Kitty's lipstick.

Ack! I looked like Betty Boop. I scraped it off.

Thirty minutes till we left. Why was I so antsy? Something was going to happen tonight. I knew it.

I went into the kitchen and wiped the counters off and washed the last supper pan and fished around for a frozen Peppermint Patty.

Fifteen minutes. I went into the living room. "Hey, Lemonhead, let's learn a new trick."

Tucker pulled himself away from his Xbox. "Can we do All the Aces?"

"Yeah," I said. "Because we *are* all the aces in this family."

By the time Annie knocked on my door to tell me it was time to go, Tucker had it mastered.

Four Tricks to Teach Tucker
Before Valentine's Day
#1 All the Aces
#2 Hotel and Motel
#3 Order, Please

#4 Vanishing Card

I gave Tucker a high five as I grabbed my purse to go.

Annie practically skipped down the hall. "I am so jazzed about this. My mom *loves* Valentine's Day. Ben is psyched. The other kids at school are psyched. Thanks for helping. It's so nice of you when you won't even be here to party with us."

"No problem."

"Can you keep the decorations and stuff at your house so my mom won't know?"

"Of course I'll keep it," I said. "Hey—can we stop at Safeway? And can you keep some ingredients at your house for a few days?"

"Sure," she nodded. "What for?"

I laughed. "A *very* special dinner."

Twenty minutes later we off-loaded from the Meyers' rental car. "I'll wait up front for you girls," Mr. Meyer said. He looked lighter tonight. Like he'd been sleeping. And smiling. And maybe winning at the computer games my dad had left him.

"Okay, do you want streamers?" I asked Annie. This time I was taking *her* by the hand around the store.

She nodded. "And balloons. And those little lacy things."

"Doilies?"

"Yes, that's it, doilies. What about the middle of the tables?"

"Bowls of flowers," I said. "I think the volunteers will help me with that. You can help me plan what you want them to look like. And I think every woman should have a corsage."

"Ooh, I like that," Annie said. "Roses."

I threw some candy into the cart. "You have to have candy," I said.

"No, *you* have to have candy," she replied.

I giggled but left the bag in the cart. She was right.

"Valentine's candy only comes once a year," I said.

"Yeah, and then there's Easter, and the Fourth of July, and Halloween. . . ."

We got some pretty napkins and plates. "We can talk about music at home," I said.

"Can we go over to the fabric?" she asked. "I want to find something really nice to make a special head cover for that night."

"Sure." I wheeled past the notions department. "I bet you didn't know I know what notions are," I teased.

Annie walked up and down the fabric aisles again, in her element. I felt pulled to the you-know-what.

This time the bolt was back in place. I slipped my hand between the gentle folds of fabric. It looked soft—and sophisticated.

"Perfect!" Annie came up behind me. "A red velvet head wrap."

I didn't want to let go of the bolt. I didn't hand it over.

"Are you okay?" she asked me.

My eyes filled with tears. "No." I hugged the fabric.

"Do you want to tell me?"

I looked over at her dad. He was reading the newspaper.

"He's fine; we've got time," she said. "My mom is sleeping and reading. We're in no rush."

We sat on the floor right in the middle of the fabric forest of bolts.

I told her about the doll, about how my mom had always wanted that dress, and how she'd never forgotten that.

"All of a sudden it's really important for me that she has that dress," I said. "It seems so important. I can't let it go. But how can I buy it for her? It'll never look just like the one on her doll, even if I find a red velvet dress somewhere."

Annie nodded and fingered the fabric. "I can try to make the dress for your mom. After all, you're helping me make my mom's party come true."

I pulled myself from my slump. "You can? Before we leave? We're only going to be here for—" I calculated the days on my fingers till February 12—"a little over two more weeks."

Annie sighed. "I can try. I don't know what the dress looks like, but if you can look through the patterns with me and find one that looks close, we can try."

"Oh, Annie, that would be so, so fantastic."

"I'd have to stop work on your shirt. It wouldn't be done," she warned.

"That's okay," I said. I stood up. "Is there enough fabric left?" Drat those ladies who had bought it up last week.

Annie tossed the bolt into the cart. "Let's go look at the patterns and see what we can find."

The blood rushed to my head. This was it! This was going to be *so* much better than the Hustle—sorry, Dad—or the airplane ride—sorry, Tucker. It was something Mom never even thought to ask for but really, really wanted. The fabric and notions would probably take up almost all the rest of my Christmas money, but that didn't matter to me. Mom *had* to have the dress.

We paged through the pattern packets. "I think this is close," I said excitedly. "And then I'll sneak the doll out of the apartment so you can change it to make it exact."

"If I can," Annie said. "I'm worried that you're not

going to like what I do. What if I mess it up and you're counting on me?"

"You won't," I answered. But we did buy out the last of the fabric, so if she messed up we were cooked.

My mom used to be a size twelve. Now, after the treatments, she was a size eight. Annie wouldn't measure Mom, just make it true to size.

We grabbed everything we needed, including the tiny brass buttons that the doll's dress had and the slick satin ribbon that tied around the waist. It would be a perfect match.

On the way home we stopped at Safeway, and I grabbed a bucket of Parmesan and a gallon of cream—okay, not exactly a gallon—and some bacon. Life was looking good.

When we got back to Anderson House, Annie sneaked the carbonara stuff into her refrigerator and I sneaked the party stuff under my bed. I planned to bring the doll over on Monday when my mom went for her final test.

Secrets were afoot.

CHAPTER NINE

Tucker and I got up early Monday morning. It was weird. Dad was still here. He hadn't gone back to Leavenworth last night.

"She's at the end of the treatment," Tucker said. "It should be the easiest time now, right? So why would he stay?"

"He said he got some extra time off," I answered.

"He *has* no time left, remember? That's why

he's been commuting." Tucker pursed his lips and took his clothes into the bathroom to change. After he closed and locked the door behind him, I got dressed myself. Something was bothering me. I pushed the fear aside and went to grab my notebook to take to school.

Hey—where was it? I rummaged through my underwear drawer, but it was nowhere to be found. My journal was missing, and with it the lists that Mom had given me.

Tucker. He probably took them. I had a good mind to read through his notebooks right now while he had the bathroom door locked.

Before I could act on the temptation, Tucker came out and we both left the bedroom. Mom and Dad were standing in the living room. "You guys going to start walking up the hill?" I asked.

"I think we're going to drive," Dad said, firmly placing his hand behind Mom's back.

"Oh." I knew Mom loved to do that walk because she got some fresh air. I wasn't going to cause a fuss, though. "You're coming home tonight, right?"

Dad nodded. "Yes, Tiger Lily. I'm going to be here all week."

"So G Kitty isn't coming back at all?"

Dad shook his head. "No. We just decided that last night."

My fettuccine carbonara plan curdled.

"But we're going to their house on Thursday night so Mom can visit with Grandpa Doug," Dad said. "It'll be good family time."

I smiled. "Wouldn't it be nice if we brought dinner to them?" I asked. "Since she's done all the cooking here?"

"Mom will be getting her strength back now that the treatments have stopped, but she's still going to be having those tests this week. She'll be too tired to cook."

"I could do it," I said.

"*You?*" Tucker and Dad said at the same time.

"We don't want M&M's casserole," Dad said.

I gave him a rock-hard stare.

All of a sudden the years dropped away from Mom's face and she started to laugh. "I think it's a great idea. Quinn, do you happen to know something special G Kitty likes to eat?"

"Oh yes, I remember what you told me, Mom," I said. I started laughing with her.

"I'll tell her that we'll do the dinner when she calls to ask how the tests went," Mom said. "But I won't tell her who is cooking. Or what. You let me know what you need us to buy."

At that, Dad steered her out the door and Tucker and I started the walk down the hallway to Fitzschool. I was so glad that we could leave on a happy note.

Wouldn't G Kitty be surprised?

As soon as we were out of earshot, I said to Tucker, "All right. Hand them over."

He looked at me as if my Ferris wheel was stuck at the top. "What are you talking about?"

"My journal and lists. The ones that were in my underwear drawer."

"I would rather be dipped in a bath of hot sulphuric acid, then coated in tar and rolled into a pack of insane porcupines before I'd go into your underwear drawer. I do not have your journal or your lists."

He stalked off to the primary classroom.

I went upstairs feeling very much like an insane porcupine. Where *were* they?

Annie had saved a seat for me. "What's wrong?" she asked as soon as I sat down.

"I'll tell you after school," I said. "If I think about it now I won't be able to concentrate."

I wondered if G Kitty had gotten into them. If she did—and she saw the part about my wanting to be kissed? I couldn't deal with it.

During group later that morning, I drifted in and out. Annie seemed more interested in Ben, to her left, than in me, to her right, which was just fine with me anyway.

After group she whispered to me, "I'm going to have coffee with Ben and his sister after lunch today.

I'll call you when I get home and you can bring over the doll."

I nodded. I'd have to watch Tucker till Mom and Dad got back from the hill.

It seemed strange. I wouldn't be going to Mom's treatment today. There was no treatment. This one, anyway, was over. Now we just had a few tests to see how successful it was and then—home sweet home!

Tucker wouldn't talk with me all the way down the hallway and back to the apartments. I was starting to believe that he was innocent. Since I had no proof either way, I wasn't particularly nice or mean.

About an hour after we got home, Annie called. "All clear?"

"Yep," I said.

"Bring the doll over. I don't want to meet you in the lobby in case your parents come home. My mom is up the hill having her Monday treatment, and my dad went with her."

Wow. Her dad went, too! "I'll be right over," I said.

I snuck the doll out of Mom's drawer. I noticed a packet in her drawer that said Treatment Prognosis. It was in a sealed envelope.

I left it there. Someone in this household had to have some integrity and not read what belonged to others.

"I'll be back," I said to Tucker. He sat on the floor,

struggling with the card trick book and the cards. It didn't look like he was getting whatever he was trying to get.

I raced down the hall. Annie was waiting for me when I reached her apartment. She hurried me into her room. Since her mom wasn't there, we figured it was okay. "My dad will be back in a little bit, so I want to sketch this out before he gets back. So you can be gone."

I nodded.

"Tell me what was going on in class today," she said.

I sat there cross-legged while she made some sketches with pencil on the dress pattern.

"You see, I have these lists," I started.

"I noticed," Annie said. She smiled. It was good to have a friend—besides Holly—who understood me.

"Anyway, my mom gave me some of the lists she had written when she was a teenager, and I kept them in my journal with mine. All of the lists are important to me. I don't know why. I guess because they help me feel like I have some, I don't know . . ." I trailed off.

"Control?" Annie suggested before turning the doll over to see the back of the dress.

"Yeah, that's it. I can set a goal and make it and plan something and it will happen. And just because they're fun."

Annie nodded and kept sketching.

"Two of the lists were especially important to me. One was a list that my mom wrote a long time ago, like twenty years or more, about stuff she wanted to do before she died."

At that, Annie set her pencil and the pattern down. "Oh, Quinn," she said. "Did she just give that to you?"

Tears filled my eyes. I nodded but I didn't trust myself to speak for a while. Finally I spoke up. "One other one that was really important was my list of things I wanted to do this year. With, ah, my mom. Kind of."

Annie nodded again but said nothing. People on Planet Cancer quickly learn when to talk and when to be quiet.

"Why was that list so important?" she finally asked.

I couldn't help it then, I started to bawl. "I just want her to see me as a woman before she goes. I just want her to see me as a woman like her." I squeezed my eyes tight, but it couldn't dam the tears.

Annie started crying, too, and hugged me. "You don't know what tomorrow will bring," she said. "The treatment may have done her a lot of good."

I nodded. That was true. "But if it didn't, then I don't know. I don't know where my hope will be. Where my love will go. If my faith will stand."

We sat there for a minute, and then Annie got up

and got me a box of tissues.

"Hey," I said, wanting to turn the topic from me to her. "How was coffee with Tall, Dark, and Handsome?"

"Well, Tall and Handsome anyway," she said. Ben was a strawberry blonde. "It was great. He asked me what he should wear to the Valentine's party and gave me his email address. His sister is so nice. Oh!" She jumped up. "That reminds me." She came back with a coffee. "It's a hazelnut white chocolate mocha with extra whipped cream."

I almost dropped my teeth. "How did you know about *that*? It's on my coffee list."

Annie grinned and blushed. "Well, I don't want you to think I was spying, but the other day when we were praying at the Sanctuary and you were reading in your journal, I peeked out of one eye because I couldn't figure out why someone would be reading and praying at the same time. I still don't know what you were doing, but I did see the list of coffee drinks and that this was one that wasn't crossed off."

My mouth dropped open. She must have thought I was angry.

"I didn't see anything else, I promise!" she said. "I wasn't trying to read your private stuff. It took me by surprise."

"No, that's not it." I shook my head. "It's just that I remember now where my journal and lists are. I stuffed them into the front pocket of my backpack that day and haven't taken them out since." My stomach felt bully-punched. I had blamed Tucker, and even G Kitty. The stress was eating up my grace.

"I got almost everything organized for the party," I told her. "The volunteers will buy the rest of the stuff you need, but you'll have to be here to set it up and to keep in touch with them the last few days. Set up the rec room, put everything where it goes."

Annie looked stricken.

"I'll leave a list for you," I said. "You can do it."

She relaxed. "Okay, I'd better get working on the dress. It doesn't look easy."

Now I felt stricken.

"Don't worry, I can do it." She shooed me, and the doll, out of the apartment.

I ran back to our apartment and into my bedroom, then yanked open the zipper on the small compartment on the front of my backpack. Sure enough, my journal was stuck deep inside.

I sighed. I opened up my notebook; everything was as I'd left it. I set the lists from Mom aside and thumbed through the pages. First, the coffee list.

I crossed off the white chocolate mocha. A list completed! Yahoo. It always gave me a good feeling. I'd celebrate with a special dessert tonight.

Quinn's List of Drinks I Must Have While
in Seattle, Before My Starbucks Card
Runs Out of Credit

#1 ~~Hazelnut white chocolate mocha with
extra whipped cream~~

#2 ~~Green Tazo tea with two packs of raw
sugar~~

#3 ~~Chantico Drinking Chocolate~~

#4 ~~Double espresso. Straight up.~~

I turned to another list. Tucker's.

"Hey, Lemonhead," I said, walking over to the corner of the living room where he sat with his cards in disarray. "Can we talk?"

He nodded.

I sat down next to him, crisscrossing my legs. "I'm sorry for accusing you of taking my lists today. I misplaced them. I was wrong to accuse you."

He looked up. "That's okay."

"No, it's not, and I'm sorry."

He looked up at me. "Have you been crying?"

I nodded. I had, with Annie. It still showed.

"You want to help me figure out how to do this card trick?" he asked. It was his way of letting me know that all was well.

"I'd love to," I said. "Which one do you want to work on?"

"Hotel and Motel," he said.

Within half an hour we had it beat. I raised my hand and he slapped it, hard, in a high five.

Four Tricks to Teach Tucker
Before Valentine's Day

#1 ~~All the Aces~~
#2 ~~Hotel and motel~~
#3 Order, Please
#4 Vanishing Card

After helping Tucker with the card trick, I worked on some homework and emailed the florist in Leavenworth. I had come up with a great scheme—different colored roses. Not just your standard red and white but also cream and peach and lavender and even navy blue. I thought about green, but that was just plain corny.

Then I ordered a whole bunch of fresh petals that would be delivered at the same time. The youth could package them up in tiny silk bags and give them as gifts or scatter them across the tables. After the party people could take them home and put them under their pillows for all I cared! The main thing was, the room was going to look—and smell—beautiful, and the flower sale was going to raise a lot of money for the Mexico missions trip this summer. Of course, we'd had to take some money out of our youth group fund to pay for the flowers in the first place, but we'd gotten a good deal; one of the moms had scouted out the best prices with me before I'd left town. I knew we'd make it all back with lots left over for the missions trip.

I sent an email to Holly.

> Hey! Don't make any plans for February 13! We'll need every girl in youth group to make the corsages out of the roses and baby's breath and to package the petals. I'm going to arrange to pick up the silk bags and have the flowers delivered to the church that day. We can all get pizza and listen to music and put them together. Can you make sure everybody saves the day?

Then I just wrote some general stuff and asked how Adam was, and the others, of course. I wished I was in school with them. I wished I was going to worship with them at youth group this week. I wished I was home.

"Can I please use the computer?" Tucker asked.

I scooted off and let him get on. I went into my room and checked out the window to see if Mom and Dad's car was driving home yet. Not yet! What was taking so long?

I heard a whoop in the living room and ran out. "What's up?"

Tucker grinned. "I'll tell you at dinner."

I started walking like I was going to look at the computer screen and he practically draped his body across it to hide it from me. "Back off, bucko!" he said.

I laughed and did. Soon thereafter I saw Mom and Dad's car coming down the hill toward Anderson House. Some strange, tiny flakes were falling from the sky. Snow? Here?

"Let's walk to dinner," Dad said as they came into the house.

"But it's snowing out!" I said.

"Exactly," Mom said. "I love a good weather event."

I couldn't tell by her face if the tests had gone well or not. She never held back for long. She'd tell me in her own time.

We walked to a steak house, and Mom ordered a whole steak and a baked potato. I ordered chicken strips and so did Tucker. Dad ordered prime rib.

"So how did the tests go?" Tucker asked.

"Tucker!" I said and threw a piece of my roll at him.

"Manners, please," Mom said sharply.

Hey! I was only trying to protect her.

"They just started a few today," Mom said. "We should know by Thursday. But so far everything seems okay."

Dad looked at her out of the corner of his eye but said nothing. I said nothing. Planet Cancer felt like it was crowding in again. Mom buttered a piece of her roll and ate it.

Tucker whipped his papers out. "Well, guess what I have?"

"I can't guess. Tell me," Mom said.

"An invitation from Making Memories. For you and me. To fly a plane."

Dad dropped his knife on the floor. I stopped chewing. Mom started to choke on her iced tea.

"What?" she said.

Tucker opened up his paper. "Making Memories is this place that grants wishes to people with breast cancer. I wrote to them and told them that you wanted to fly a plane and they said *yes!*"

"Let me see that," Dad said. Tucker handed the paper over to him. As he read it, he burst out in a grin. "You really did something great, Tuck," Dad said. "But why flying a plane?"

"Mom wanted to do that," Tucker said. Dad looked at Mom in surprise.

"It's true," she said and looked at me. I winked at her. I knew she remembered the list when she winked back.

"We can go in the beginning of March, at Boeing Field. You'll have a few hours of instruction and then you'll go up with the instructor—and me—and get to take the controls."

"The control is *mine!*" Mom joked kind of loudly. The people at the table next to us tossed a strange look in our direction. I wanted to stick my tongue out at them. I didn't care what anyone thought. My mom was happy!

We all laughed and ate our fill.

I whispered to Tucker, "Remind me later to tell you what I have planned for Thursday night. You can help."

"At G Kitty's?" he asked.

I nodded and grinned. He grinned back. He knew mischief was afoot.

I ordered the cappuccino mudslide for dessert to celebrate completing my coffee list.

After our full meal we walked home, catching snowflakes on our tongues and eyelashes. Mom made the first snowball and dropped it down Dad's back. You should have seen him wriggle and move. "Hey!" he cried out.

"Who says you can't dance?" Mom teased.

Tucker grabbed one and pitched it at me, and I threw a tiny one right back. Dad got Mom in the back with a soft snowball and she laughed out loud.

We quieted down and held hands; as we got closer to Anderson House I looked at the landscape.

The crocuses still tried to push their heads through

the hard ground. Only a few days ago Annie and I had walked on this exact path and the flowers seemed to be winning. Today, though, an untimely frost had taken some of them.

CHAPTER TEN

Dinner for me? What a surprise." I could see G Kitty trying to peek into the Safeway bags, but Tucker and I held them fast. "What will it be?"

"Now, Ma, go and take a rest," Mom said, her eyes twinkling. "It's not every day that someone cooks for you!"

"Do you need me to get the vegetable chopper out?" she asked.

"No," Grandpa Doug said. Mom must have

filled him in. I gave him a quick kiss on the cheek and a hug and shooed him out of the room, too. I think they went into the living room to play dominoes or bridge or something while Tucker and I cooked. G Kitty brought out her massage oil, so I knew Mom was in for a treat, too.

"You can make the breadsticks," I told Tucker. He banged the container on the edge of the counter till it popped open, then unwound the worm-like breadstick dough and put the pieces on a cookie sheet.

In the meantime I got the water boiling. I poured the cream into a large saucepan and turned it on warm. Then I added the butter and stirred in some cheese till it was warm and gooey. I broke the already-cooked bacon into bits and stirred it in, too.

"How many fat grams do you think are in here?" Tucker dipped his pinky into the sauce and smacked his lips.

"About a thousand," I said. We both giggled. Tucker dropped the noodles into the water, put the breadsticks into the oven, and set the table in the dining room. I cut up some tomatoes—the one vegetable allowed, and only because the recipe called for it.

"Sooey!" Tucker called.

I smacked him on the behind with the colander. "Can you please call them to the table nicely?"

He draped a towel over his arm like a high-class

waiter and went into the living room. "Dinnah is served," he said.

When they sat down, I brought out a steaming platter of noodles tossed and sauced, and Tucker brought out the breadsticks. Dad had poured water into the crystal glasses. Every eye looked at G Kitty.

"Oh," she said. Then nothing else. It was quiet for a long time. I started to feel uncomfortable. I wanted to tease her but not hurt her.

"It's fettuccine carbonara," I said.

"Yes," she answered. "I used to love it."

I passed the platter around and everyone took some. I leaned over to G Kitty. "You can sprinkle some bran on it or something if you want."

"No, no."

We slurped it up, and it was really, truly good. G Kitty had a second helping, but I was pretty sure it was just to make sure I wasn't hurt. She was fussy, but she was a good grandma.

Mom smiled at me, widely, and kicked me lightly under the table. I knew then that it was all right.

Later that night I tossed and turned in the lavender bedroom. Mom still had the Andy Gibb poster up. I thought he looked wimpy with his hair feathering over to one side. And it looked like he had make-up on! Did girls really crush on him when Mom was young?

I went to get a glass of milk; maybe it would help

me sleep. When I got to the kitchen, though, the refrigerator door was open. G Kitty was caught red-handed, fork in the leftover fettuccine.

I grinned. G Kitty grinned. She took an even bigger forkful and chewed with relish. "This is so good. I had forgotten how good it was," she said. "It's one of the nicest things you could have done."

I stood still. "I have to admit something," I said. "I did it to pester you."

She got a clean fork and stuck it in for another bite. "I know. Where do you think you got that spunk from?"

"My mom." I smiled again.

"And just where do you think *she* got it from?" G Kitty jerked her thumb back toward herself. "Me. This is the best fettuccine carbonara I have ever tasted. Much better than I have ever made." At that, she kissed me on the forehead and I gave her a big squeeze good-night.

I walked back upstairs and heard the sound of my parents giggling in the spare bedroom. I turned my back to Andy Gibb and opened my journal to the page with my New Year's list.

Quinn's New Year's Resolutions

#1 Help mom stay healthy.

#2 Drive a car before any of my friends. I

am not kidding. Otherwise I will ONCE AGAIN be last since all my friends will turn 15 before I do. I just want to be first, at one thing that is important, for once.

#3 ~~make an unhealthy meal that Grandma Kitty says tastes delicious.~~

#4 Get kissed by a boy. Not Tucker.

Would Valentine's Day hold the key to number four?

The next morning we drove home. Tucker and I were playing hooky from school, but that was okay.

When we got home, there was a message on the phone for my mom. It was from Mercy, Annie's mom. "Mary, please call me as soon as you can." Her voice sounded tense. Almost desperate.

Mom took the phone into her bedroom and called Mercy back. They talked for about fifteen minutes and then Mom came back into the room. "Mercy has the flu," she said. She sat down on the couch.

"Oh no," my dad said. We knew what that meant. If you get sick when you're on chemotherapy, the doctor might decide to stop treatment. Chemo kills off your body's ability to fight infection, so you can't always take it if you're sick. But if you stop the chemo before the full treatment is over, the chance of it completely killing the cancer isn't as good. Maybe she'd had enough already. Or maybe not. Maybe it was erased. Or maybe it would stick around or come back.

"Are they stopping chemo?" Dad asked, and Mom nodded.

"Didn't she get a flu shot?" I asked. We all got flu shots because of having cancer patients around.

"Yes," Mom said. "They all did. So it won't be as bad on her or last as long as it could have. But still."

"Let's pray for her," Dad said. We sat around the couch and prayed for Mercy and for Annie and for Annie's dad, whose name, I learned, was Gunther.

Afterward my mom answered her other messages. "They want me to come to the hospital for a CAT scan and maybe an MRI on Monday," she told my dad. My dad looked like he was going to cry.

"Why?" I asked.

"The last bit of testing from this treatment," Mom said firmly. I recognized that voice. It meant end of topic, end of discussion.

"We talk about everything!" I said.

"Yes, we do," Mom said. "And we'll talk about this, too. When we have all the facts."

I went into my room and took the phone with me. I called Annie.

"Hey," I said after she answered the phone. "How are you doing?"

"Not good," she said. "My mom is sick. She has to stop the chemo for at least a week."

"Maybe she's had enough so that it'll be okay," I said.

"Yeah. Maybe," Annie answered. "I have some good news, though."

"What?"

"I told my dad about Sun-Hea. . . ."

"And?"

"And he was really happy. And proud of me for taking action! I know he wants to see her. I do, too. We'll tell my mom after she gets well again from this flu and we forget all about cancer and move on with life."

"Okay," I said. I was glad there weren't any secrets between her and her dad anymore.

"I told my mom about the party to cheer her up. It was the happiest I've seen her since we've been here. She loves Valentine's Day, and for her to think that I was going to make sure she had a party in her honor, with everyone else here, she said it was just the nicest gift."

"I'm so glad," I said. "I'll make sure everything is set up before I leave. You'll have to send me some pictures."

"I will," Annie said. "It means so much to me that you're doing the work for the party. I'm making progress on your mom's dress. I should get quite a bit done. I can't go to school anyway. They don't want me to infect anyone else in case I am contagious, and my dad is busy taking care of my mom."

"Oh," I said. I didn't know what else to say. I didn't want to profit from her mom's sickness, even though I wanted my mom's dress to get done.

"I'm praying for you," I said.

I hung up the phone and went out into the living room. My mom was typing away on the computer. When I came near, she turned the screen off.

"Whatcha doin'?" I asked.

"Writing back to Mercy," Mom said. "Shoo."

Annie's mom had emailed her? Mom wrote a long, long email back. Maybe when Mercy felt good enough to read something, the email would cheer her up.

I stayed up late finishing *The Return of the King*. I'd read it before, of course, but the way that victory was snatched out of defeat always lifts me up.

We had the best weekend ever. Dad made chocolate chip pancakes and we lounged in our jammies for hours. We made a Make-Your-Own-Opoly game with our family. I got one side of the board; so did Tucker, Dad, and Mom. Mom got the side where Boardwalk would have been. Tucker named all of his spaces after elements on the periodic table. Weird.

We drove to a church in Seattle and sat together, all four of us, and sang and listened. Even though it was a little boring, I was glad to be together.

I was counting the days until we could go home.

Monday came soon.

"I'm going up the hill for a few final tests," Mom said as she brushed mascara on her lashes. "I should be back by the time you guys get back from school."

School dragged without Annie. I chatted with Ben after group.

"Is Annie doing okay?" he asked. I said she was. She'd been gone on Friday, too, and he hadn't known why.

"Can you give this to her from me?" He handed me a note. I promised I would and tucked it into my backpack, unread. Annie was quarantined from school, but she could at least meet me at her apartment door. I'd have to be careful. I didn't want to catch the flu and ruin my own Valentine's Day.

When I got home, Mom still wasn't back. Dad was home, waiting for Tucker.

"What's going on?" I asked.

"Unexpected tests," Dad answered.

I was going to ask him if I should go up and visit. But then he'd probably say no and I'd have to disobey. "I'm going to bring something to Annie," I said. I didn't say where else I was going.

I took the phone into my bedroom and called Annie. "Can I bring something by?" I asked her.

"In half an hour," she said. "My hands hurt. My arms hurt. I think it's from sewing too much. I could use a break."

"Okay," I said. "I have a note for you from Ben."

"Oh-kay!" she said. I smiled and went to check for an email from Adam. There was one!

> *Everything's ready. Are you coming home soon? I hope so. It almost seems like you don't live here anymore.*
>
> *Love,*
Adam

Bad Point: It seems to him like I don't live there anymore.

Good Points: He wants me to come home soon. Everything is arranged. He signed it "Love."

Woo-hoo!

Today was Monday the sixth. I'd be home on Sunday the twelfth. Six days and counting.

I brought the note to Annie's apartment. "Are you doing okay?" I asked.

She nodded. "My mom seems to be getting better. I am just so tired. I think I've been worried, plus working hard on my homework and also on your mom's dress. I have a lot of the big pieces done, but the little handwork is what's going to take some time, and that's what I don't have done. I have almost a week, though. I'll get it done before you go."

"Thank you," I said. "Anyway, here's your note. I didn't read it." I handed the note over to her. She slipped it, unread, into her pocket.

"I know you wouldn't. Where are you going?"

"Up the hill."

Annie looked surprised. "Is your mom there today? I thought her treatment was done."

"It is. She's having some extra tests. I thought she might want some company."

"Should I, um, should I pray for you?" Annie asked. "For her?"

"Yes, please!" I said. In spite of my fear, I was so glad that Annie felt like she wanted to talk with God. She thought of it on her own.

I walked up the hill. My mom's name was still listed on the room. The door was closed.

I stopped outside of the door. Maybe my mom wouldn't want anyone else in there. All of a sudden I heard a tremendous noise.

"*All* I want to *do* is finish what I have *started!*" a shout came. Then a crash, like someone throwing something.

I heard crying. My mom. I heard another voice in there. A doctor? A nurse?

Suddenly I ran. I turned my back and ran down

the hall. I bypassed the elevator to run down the stairs, then down the hill. I could hear my own breath in my head, and I had a cramp in my side, like I had when we'd tested in P.E. The sweat and slight mist of the day slicked my hair to my scalp.

What was going on in there? Was my mom talking about Ribbons in the Snow again? What else did she want to finish? Why couldn't she?

It just couldn't be good. Nothing could be all right anymore.

I sat on the bench outside of Anderson House long enough to make sure that I was pulled together before going inside and up to our apartment.

When I opened the door, I looked at Dad. He knew something. I could tell by the look on his face. When my mom first got cancer, though, the doctors told us that it was best if the patient was in control of who knew what and when. So we sat there, all of us, saying nothing, waiting for Mom.

Dad played computer games. Tucker shuffled cards. I went into my room and sat on the window seat. My cross suncatcher was on my window. I ripped it down. I wanted nothing to do with God.

As I sat on the window seat, one last ray of sunlight popped through the Seattle dusk, beaming through my window and painting pink and purple over all of the gray. I knew it was the Lord. I yielded to it, and it warmed me. My breathing slowed down. The light beam lasted an unusually long time.

Even if I wanted nothing to do with Him, He still wanted me. "*Help me,*" I whispered.

A quick knock sounded on the door and Tucker came into our room. "Will you help me with a card trick?"

I sighed. "Of course. Bring them here." I guess a distraction was a help in its own way.

We sat on my bed and learned Order, Please. Even I had to laugh when Tucker burped and called it, "Odor, Please."

Four Tricks to Teach Tucker
Before Valentine's Day

#1 ~~All the Aces~~
#2 Hotel and Motel
#3 ~~Order, Please~~
#4 ~~Vanishing Card~~

Mom came home later and said nothing. She didn't look like she'd just thrown a big fit a few hours ago. I was going to do like we'd all learned to do—let her be in charge of telling us what was going on with her cancer. She said she'd get some test results back by the end of the week and then we'd all talk—and go home to Leavenworth and enjoy life. That's exactly what she said—enjoy life! My spirits soared.

After school Tuesday, Annie called me.

"How are you doing?" she asked. "How is your mom?"

"Okay," I said. I shut the door and quietly told her about the incident at the hospital yesterday.

"I understand," she said. "I have good news and bad news." Her voice sounded weary.

"What's the good news?" I asked.

"I met your God yesterday."

I was startled. "What happened?"

"After you left I decided to pray for you right away. I wanted to leave the apartment, but I'm quarantined. Good thing I didn't, anyway. More on that in a minute."

She gulped a breath. "So I went into my room and closed the door and sat on the window seat for a long time. Maybe like half an hour. I was praying for you, and then all of a sudden I thought, how do I know any of this matters? If it's even real? So I asked God, 'Are you even there? Who are you?'"

I was caught up in her story. "Did He answer you?" I asked.

"Yes," she said. "In a clever and unique way. As I

was sitting there, a beam of light burst through the clouds, and all of a sudden it came right through the suncatcher. It lit up my whole room with golden light. It was the only bright thing in the room. The cross. I knew then who God was. Jesus. And that He was for me.

"It felt good to pray for you, Quinn," she went on, "like you've prayed for me. And now I will always have God with me, even if I don't know what else lies ahead."

She was quiet. "You do think that was God, don't you?"

The tears rolled down my face. "Yes, Annie, I know it was."

"Now the bad news," she added quietly after a minute. "I'm sick."

"I'm sorry," I said. "I worried about that. The flu?"

"Yes," she said. "I'm so tired. I thought I was achy from sewing, but it's sore muscles from the flu. I am getting worse every day. Quinn—" She took a deep breath. "Quinn, there's more. I can't finish the dress."

I sat there on the phone, my complete joy over the confirmation from God that He was with us both crushed by this news. "Are you sure?" I asked.

"I'm sure," she said. "I'm so very sorry. You don't have to do anything else on my party because it's not fair. My mom will be well enough by then. But I don't even know if I can go. I have to wait till every sign of sickness is gone or I could infect someone. It's in seven days. I don't know if I'll be okay."

"Oh yes, you will!" I tried to hold back the tears and think of her and not Mom's dress. "I'm almost done with your party stuff. I can finish up before I go home."

"Quinn," Annie said quietly, "your grandma might be able to finish the dress."

"She has arthritis," I said.

"I know. But she's not sick and I am. I could barely get out of bed today. Even if this flu is gone in a few days, there won't be enough time to get the dress done by Sunday when you go home."

"It's okay," I said. "Take care of yourself." I hung up the phone.

I sat on my bed, hands in my lap. What was happening in my life? I got out my notebook and found the right list.

Things I Will Pray for Annie

#1 ~~That she will find Jesus waiting for her~~
#2 ~~That she will meet Sun-Hea~~
#3 That she will make peace with her mom having cancer
#4 That her parents will fall in love again

Thank you, God, for answering this prayer. You are so good.

I put the suncatcher back up on my window and smiled. Now Annie truly *was* one of us. And I didn't mean just my group!

Call her. I felt the voice in my heart. *Call her,* it nudged me.

Annie? No. I knew whom He meant.

I picked up the phone and dialed. "Grandma Kitty? Do you have a minute to talk?"

Later that night, I didn't tell anyone who I was meeting in the lobby—not Mom, of course, but also not Dad, not Tucker. Only Annie knew, and that's because she had to send her dad down to the lobby with the sewing machine, the dummy, and the material all neatly folded in an under-the-bed cardboard box.

After Mr. Meyer dropped it off, I just sat there, waiting. Me and the nighttime front desk guy. About nine o'clock he buzzed them in.

I stood up and hugged them both, then drew them into the rec room.

"Thanks for driving down, and for keeping it a secret," I said. "Here's the dress." I had already explained on the phone that Annie had started the dress but had gotten sick and couldn't finish in time. "It's really important to me to get it done. Can you do it, G Kitty?" I pleaded.

"I don't know, dear. My hands are so bad I can barely hold a pen anymore."

"I know," I said. "Annie said she got all of the big pieces sewn, so it's just the smaller details that need to be sewed on."

"Let me see it," G Kitty said. I opened the box and she took the pieces out and started to cry. "Oh dear, my dear. The red velvet dress."

I put my arm around her. "I didn't want to hurt your feelings."

She shook her head. "No, I was wrong then. I just wanted things to be *right* so much. I worried what people would think." She sniffed and brought a hankie to her eyes and then looked over the fabric. "I've been a poor mother in so many ways."

"No you haven't," I said. I let her sniffle for a minute before asking again. "Can you do it, G Kitty? Can you?"

She looked it over. "I will try. If it takes everything left in my hands, I will try. Velvet is just so hard to work with. The small pieces are harder on my hands. I could so easily make a mistake."

I nodded. That's what Annie had said, too.

Grandpa Doug took it all out to the car. "We've got to get back on the road." I knew it would be close to midnight when they got home.

I stood by the door with G Kitty, our arms around each other.

"What are you eating?" she said. Drat. I had tried to hide my candy bar, but it peeked out of my pocket.

"A candy bar," I said quietly.

"Give that to me," she said. I handed it over. I didn't want to upset her now that she was going to try to sew.

She took the candy bar—a super size one—from my hand and ripped some more of the wrapper off. Then she took a huge bite, chewed it with relish, swallowed, and licked her lips. "Want a bite before I take the rest of this to eat on the way home? I need to keep my strength up now, you know."

I started laughing and took a bite. She wrapped it back up, tucked it into her pocket, and winked as Grandpa Doug came to escort her to the waiting car.

"See you soon," he said, a secret glimmer in his eye.

Now, what did *that* mean?

CHAPTER ELEVEN

I was pretty sure that Mom knew what the test results were, because she got a call early Friday morning and then she and Dad shut themselves up in the bedroom and talked. Tucker and I went to school, and when we came home Mom and Dad sat us down.

I looked at Tucker. He looked at me. We thought this was going to be the big test result news.

"Dad and I have planned a fun weekend,"

Mom said instead. "We don't get to Seattle very often, and now that the treatment phase is over and I have some strength back, we'd like to do some fun things before we go home."

"Okay," Tucker said. We both wanted to ask Mom about the cancer, but we both abided, for the moment, by the fact that it was best if the patient got to share her own news when she wanted. "What do we get to do?"

"Tonight, we'll check into a hotel," Mom said. "Because I want to swim and I haven't had a chance to swim for a long time. One of the hotels downtown has an indoor rooftop pool."

"Hooray!" Tucker loves to swim. I think swimming's okay, but I knew my mom loved it so I'd go along for her.

"Tomorrow is girls' and guys' day," Dad continued. "Mom is kidnapping Quinn and taking her on a surprise all day. Grandpa Doug is going to come down to Seattle and do some stuff with Tucker and me. Like go to the fossil museum."

Tucker's eyes lit up. I was wary. What was with the big party atmosphere? I had to admit, though, I was curious about where Mom would take me.

"Is Grandma Kitty coming with us?" I asked.

"No." Mom looked genuinely confused. "I had told her we wanted part of the day to ourselves, but that she could join us for dinner. She said she was too busy. Too busy doing what, I wondered. That surprised me."

I knew. G Kitty had to finish the dress. It was slow going. The fine details were both the hardest to do and the hardest on her hands.

"We're still going home on Sunday, though, right?" I asked.

"We'll talk about that later," Dad said.

I opened my mouth to argue, but he shot me a look. I quieted. For now. I was *not* going to miss my Valentine's party.

Before we left for the hotel, I emailed Holly.

Everything is set for the flower delivery on Monday, so we should have time to arrange them and get them ready for sale. I made the forms that we can use at the back table and also the little verse papers. I'm still trying to think of a verse to go in the petal bags. See you soon—we're off to a hotel!

Love,
Q

I had one email in my inbox. From Adam.

Hey Q, I'm heading out to ski practice, but I

*wanted you to know we're all looking forward to
your coming home.*

> Love,
> Adam

Dad took us to the Sheraton, and we checked into an awesome suite. Tucker got a rollaway, so we didn't even have to share a bed.

Mom went into the bathroom to change into her suit. "Want to wear my swimsuit?" she asked, dangling the one with the full breast forms in front of me. I threw a ponytail holder at her, and she giggled and closed the door behind her.

Mom and Tucker swam, and I lounged and played cards with Dad. Afterward we walked downstairs to the *Chocolate Café*. No kidding. I drank a cup of gourmet hot chocolate, ate a piece of fudge cake, and sat back in pure bliss.

Later that night Mom and Dad watched an old movie and I taught Tucker the last card trick. Actually, he pretty much taught himself.

"You're ready for Tuesday," I said. "CJ is going to be so jealous."

Tucker beamed. "Oh yeah. I'm bringing the cards to school, too. Maybe I'll make some bets and then my friends will not only have Vanishing Cards, they'll have vanishing money."

"No gambling," Mom said, never taking her eyes off of the television. *How* had she heard that?

I laughed and gave Tucker a high five.

Four Tricks to Teach Tucker
Before Valentine's Day

#1 ~~All the Aces~~
#2 ~~Hotel and motel~~
#3 ~~Order, Please~~
#4 ~~Vanishing Card~~

I read for a while and then Mom said, "Better get to sleep. We have a very busy day tomorrow."

Still no word on the test results. But tomorrow something fantastic loomed. I could tell just by the way Mom looked at me.

The next morning we hauled our gear back to the apartment. Mom went to visit Mercy, Annie's mom, for just a minute. They met in the lobby, and when they came back Mom was smiling. "Mercy looks good," she told me. "Almost fully recovered and therefore not contagious anymore. They're not going to continue with this course of chemo after the flu because they think they got it all. Annie is feeling much better, too, but she's got to stay in the apartment till Tuesday morning just to make sure she's not contagious anymore."

The significance of that didn't hit me till later on in the day.

Dad pulled me into the bedroom without Mom and unwrapped a package covered with plain brown paper. A DVD fell out. *Do the Hustle! An Instructional DVD.* "I'll be practicing today for the Valentine's party at church." He smiled at me. "Don't tell Mom."

A few minutes later Grandpa Doug knocked on the door. "Hi, Grandpa Dog," I said. I hugged him and he hugged me back. He handed something to my mom, something I couldn't see, and Mom grabbed her purse. She kissed Dad, I sprayed some Tiger Lily behind my ears, and we were off.

When we got to the front of the Anderson House, I started walking toward the parking lot.

"Where are you going?" Mom asked.

"To the car."

Mom grinned and shook her head. She walked toward a long, sleek, restored Mustang parked in front of the sidewalk.

I didn't recognize it at first. It had fat, shiny black

tires, and the metal gleamed metallic purple. No kidding. It even had the fuzzy dice hanging from the rearview mirror.

"Grandpa Doug's car? We're taking Grandpa Doug's car?" I had never even seen it out of the garage.

"Mm-hmm," Mom said. "I decided it was time I drove it." Her eyes sparkled. "Grandpa Doug gave in as he never did when I was a teen and brought it down for us. I figured it would be *most* fun to drive it together, you and me. We're taking it for the day."

I leaped around the side of the car and hopped into the passenger side. When I got in, Mom handed me a pair of rhinestone-studded sunglasses, and then she put on a matching pair.

"I don't suppose there's an Andy Gibb poster in the backseat," I teased. She slapped me playfully with her gloves.

First we went to a nail salon and got our nails done. Mom's were a glossy Valentine red, and mine were wine colored. Sophisticated. Secretly I was so glad that she chose red. It would match her dress, if G Kitty got it done in time. Then we each got a heart painted on one pointer finger.

Next we went to lunch at the Georgian Room in a hotel downtown.

Mom pulled up and handed a bill to the valet, who parked our car for us.

I ordered lobster soup and mom ordered a crab salad. Our lemonade came in tiny individual carafes.

"Tucker is going to be so jealous when he finds out," I said.

"No he won't." Mom bit into another piece of bread. "I'm taking him to Boeing Field tomorrow so we can sign up for our flight lessons."

"Not too late tomorrow," I said. "I mean, we'll want to get on the road. That reminds me. We'll have to pack when we get home tonight. Will I be able to say good-bye to Annie?"

"Yes," Mom said. Then she was quiet for a moment. "Shall we get going?"

"Oh yeah," I said. "Where to?"

"Lynden," Mom said.

I stood up and folded my napkin on my empty seat. "To G Kitty's house?" Now I was puzzled. "Are we bringing Grandpa Doug home?"

"No," Mom said. "We won't even see G Kitty. Come with me."

I followed her out and the valet brought our car around again. We drove to Lynden, chatting all the way. Finally she drove off the main road and headed down past Wiser Lake out into the country roads. Dusty country roads. Grandpa Doug was going to be mad.

"We'd better get the car washed on the way into

town," I said. "Or we'll be in big trouble." I took my sunglasses off. Dusk started to powder the early evening.

"I wanted you to come here with me. This is where I learned to drive. We got such a good laugh out of that last month, I thought it would be fun for you to see me on this road. And fun for *me* to be here in this car!"

I smiled. I could imagine my mom as a gawky teenager and Grandpa Doug holding his breath as he watched her jerk down the road.

"Okay, get out," Mom said. She got out of the car. I got out, too. The view was nice here.

"Now get in on the driver's side," Mom said.

"What?" My arms started to tingle and my hair stood on end. I felt the blood rush to my face.

"You heard me. Get in the driver's seat."

My hands were shaking. Did she mean it? I had thought I would drive for the first time in the old beater truck my dad kept parked on the side of the house in Leavenworth—so that if I dinged it or whatever the damage wouldn't be too bad.

I scooted the seat up so that my feet could reach the pedals. My mind blanked.

"Which one is to go? Which one to stop?" Great. I could see the headlines now. "Underage girl drives classic car into tree by Wiser Lake."

"The pedal on the left is the brake, and the one on the right is the gas," Mom said. "You only use your right foot to drive. Stick your left foot to the side and just let it relax."

I did. Then she showed me how to hold the steering wheel. "You put your hands like this." She positioned my hands with hers on the wheel and held fast. "Then you put your foot on the brake and shift into gear like this." She moved the stick till it was in the "D" position for Drive.

"Add gas and go!" she said. She sat back, not looking nervous at all. Her confidence made me feel confident that I could handle whatever was down the road. I rolled along, slowly at first. I jerked the car a few times and stopped.

"I can't. I'm too nervous."

"You've got it!" she said. "You've got it! Keep going."

We drove up and down the country road for about fifteen minutes. "I'm ready to take it out onto the highway."

Mom laughed. "Not till you have a license, miss." She took out her cell phone and took a picture. "Now you've beat everyone, and we have the proof right here. You even beat Annie, who can drive next Thursday. I had to make sure you beat her, didn't I?"

I nodded. My face was flushed red and I was riding high. This was one of the best days of my life. We had stopped at a grocery store on the way to Lynden and bought a picnic dinner; now we went to a place overlooking the lake and sat down with it. It was chilly, but the trees protected us from the wind. Mom opened up her sandwich and I ate some chips. I just knew it was okay to ask.

"The tests weren't good, were they?"

"No, they weren't," Mom said.

Tears filled my eyes. I had known in my heart all along that something was wrong, but hearing the words out loud was so much different. It breathed life into my fears and now there was no pretending.

"It's nothing the treatment did or didn't do," Mom said. "I was feeling a little unsteady before we even got here, but we wanted to give it a try. The tests I had run last week showed a shadow on my brain."

Now the tears really rolled down my face. Mom handed me a napkin, and I brushed it against my face, glad for its harshness. I cried harder and shook, and Mom started to cry, too. She set down her sandwich and held my hands, then hugged me and we cried together.

"You know what the shadow on the brain means," she said. I nodded. It meant the cancer had gone to her brain. The last stage.

"What's the next treatment?" I asked once I was

able to stop crying long enough to talk. I hiccuped softly.

Mom sat still. We could hear the first frogs of the season croaking to one another deep in the belly of the ferns. "There aren't going to be any more treatments, Quinn. I'm done."

I stood up. "No! Mom! There have to be other things we can try."

She took my hand again and I sat down. "There are a few things I could try, but they would only give me a few months extra, or maybe a year extra, and I'd be sick and tired that whole time. That's not how I want to spend the last months of my life. I want to swim and go to the spa and shop with you and pray and fly with Tucker and love your dad. I have to choose between a good life with a shorter time or a longer time—although not much longer—with a poor quality of life. I choose a good life."

I started sobbing all over again and ripped my hand from hers and walked to the edge of the woods. *Why* was this happening to my mom? Why not some of those mean people who beat their children or ignore others' problems or steal money or whatever?

Mom let me stand there for a while and then she said, "Quinn."

I came back and sat by her. The warmth of her

body next to mine soothed me, and I cuddled up under her arm.

"Why should you get it? Why does God want you now? I need you now. Dad does. Tucker does. If God loves you so much, then why are you going to die and be robbed of your life?"

Mom sighed. "I don't have all of those answers. I do believe that I wasn't robbed of any time. I was reading in Psalm 139 that all of my days were known to Him before I had even lived one. However many years and days I live, that is the exact amount He planned for."

I couldn't accept that. "Then what good is it that we even wasted a month here?"

"It wasn't a waste to try to see if it could help. Annie isn't a waste, is she?" Mom asked. "Her mother told me that Annie has found God."

I nodded.

Mom continued. "Here's what I've learned. If God says He is everywhere, and He does, then that means that His body needs to be everywhere. If God is going to be in a cancer hospital in body as well as in spirit, then that means a Christian has to be there. Christians are His body. If God is going to be at Fitzschool in body, then that means a Christian has to be there. If God is bodily present in the suffering in India or the poorest part of a town, then His body—Christians—need to be there."

I nodded. I wished it didn't make sense. But it kind of did.

"So when I gave Him my life, Quinn, I said He could have it. And look at all the good He has allowed me in spite of it all."

She stroked my hand. "I have you. I have Dad. I have Tucker. I have friends. I started Ribbons in the Snow. Death can't rob me of those things."

"Is that what you were yelling about in the hospital the other day?" I asked. A lonely breeze skirted around us.

Mom looked genuinely surprised. "What? When?"

I explained about Monday and her saying that she just wanted to finish what she'd started.

"No, Quinn, I was talking about you and Tucker. Getting to finish what I've started with you two. I wish I could stay long enough to see you both grown and married and me be just like G Kitty." Her eyes twinkled. "Okay, not exactly."

"But you can't be here," I said.

"No, I can't."

I let the darkness fall around me.

"Do you remember what I said about feeling good that Ribbons in the Snow was a success even after I'd left it?"

I nodded. "You said that the biggest test would be if it did well without you to guide it to the finish. If the seeds you planted took root on their own."

Mom nodded. "That's true for you and Tucker, too."

I nodded and started to cry again. "How long?"

Mom hugged me and cried some more, too. "Maybe six months."

"How will we make it?" I asked. "How will we live?"

"Like we always have," Mom said. "Not ignoring the truth but not gulping down depressing things, either. 'Whatever is true . . .'"

"'. . . whatever is noble, whatever is right, whatever is pure, whatever is lovely, whatever is admirable—if anything is excellent or praiseworthy—think about such things,'" I finished for her. I had memorized that in seventh grade.

"I can never lose you," she said. "This will just be a short time apart and then I'll meet you in heaven."

I wiped my eyes. "How will I find you there when it's my turn?"

Mom sat still for a long while. "There's going to be great feasting in heaven, right?"

I nodded.

"I'll meet you at the chocolate table," she said.

I smiled through my tears. She handed a small bag to me, the tiny red velvet purse from her doll. "I want you to open this after I'm gone, but not before, okay?"

I nodded.

"We'll pray about it together every day," Mom said, reaching her arm around me.

I nodded and drew closer. I would need to pray every day if I was ever going to make it through.

"Ready to roll?" She squeezed my shoulder.

I guessed so. We drove around town because Mom wanted to get a look at all of the places where she'd grown up. When we drove past G Kitty's house, I could see her in the dining room, light still on, head bent over. She was working on the dress. Would it be ready tomorrow? We each bought a chocolate malt at the drive-through before we left town.

"Will we see G Kitty tomorrow?" I asked. "Before we go?"

"Yes, she's going to come down for an hour in the morning. Also, you'll have to say good-bye to Annie through the door."

"Oh. She can't come out till Tuesday."

"Right," Mom said.

It hit me, then. Tuesday was the party. The one at my church, but also the party Annie had planned for her mom. There was no way she could do all the last-minute arranging on Tuesday by herself. I had arranged long ago for everything to be delivered on Monday so Annie wouldn't have to rush. We'd signed contracts about it. There were flowers to be arranged and table linens to set out and food to store a day ahead of time. We were expecting about a hundred people. One tired girl—even if she wasn't contagious anymore—couldn't do it alone.

Annie had done her best to get my mom the dress. I felt like I needed to help her now, when she needed help to give her mom the party she'd always wanted. "Mom," I said. "What would you think about our staying here through Valentine's Day?"

Mom looked at me with her mouth open. "And miss the party at home?"

I sighed. I really, really didn't want to do that. "Yeah. I want to be there. You know how much I do. But I will be there on Wednesday. I can see my friends then. I know we'll have Easter at home. When Annie goes home, she won't have anyone else to help throw a party for her mom. She can't do the last details if she's stuck in her apartment. I think I need to help her."

Mom nodded slowly. "If that's what you want, I think we can convince Dad and Tucker."

"Will you be sad to miss the Valentine's party?" I asked.

Mom shook her head. "This party was always most important to *you*, honey. It will still be a party here, a dance, and tons of fun. It will be even more special since you've planned it all! Quinn, if you decide to do

225

it, you have to do it with a willing heart or Annie will feel terrible."

I swallowed. "Yes, Mom. I can do that." I would email Holly and Adam when I got home. How could one day hold such fun—driving!—and such terrible news about my mom and now a decision I had to make that didn't seem joyful at all? It was too deep to swim in. I started sinking.

When we got home, the guys were all happy, but I knew that Tucker and Grandpa Doug didn't know yet. Mom was going to tell Tucker tomorrow and Grandpa Doug and Grandma Kitty when they came down together, she'd told me. I avoided them so I wouldn't accidentally give it away by a look or a tear or anything.

"I'm taking a shower," I said. I got in and let the hot water run and then I bawled. I knew no one could hear me through the water. And if my face got all red, they'd think it was the hot water.

When I collected myself, I got on the computer and told Holly and Adam that I couldn't be there till Wednesday but that I hoped they would have a really good time without me and that maybe we could get together over the weekend. I couldn't bring myself to tell them about Mom yet. I'd do that in person.

I called Annie and told her we were staying for the

party and that I would be there to take care of all the details.

"Oh, great! Awesome," she said. "I'm sorry you can't go home on time because of your mom's tests, but I'm really glad you'll be here. And that you can finish the party! God worked it all out just right. Isn't that great? My mom will be *so* excited."

I didn't tell her that it was a choice, that we didn't have to stay. I didn't want her to feel bad that I was missing my party—because then she'd enjoy it less, or try to convince me to go.

Instead, I asked her the thing I didn't want to ask. "Do you have Michelle's email? She's on your list of people praying for you from my church."

"Sure." Annie set the phone down and went to get the paper. When she got back on, she gave me the email address.

Before hanging up, I said I'd see her on Tuesday, if she was feeling better, to organize the final details. Taking care of details was one way to forget what was going on.

I emailed Michelle.

> *Hi. You don't know me, but I am in your youth group. I heard that you don't have a job for the Valentine's party. I won't be able to come back in time, and I was wondering if you wanted to do the*

flowers. Please email me back and let me know
and I will send all the information
                              Quinn

Mom came to tuck me in just as I pulled the little red bag and my journal out of my purse. I put the bag gently on my bed, opened my journal, and turned to the page with my New Year's list on it.

Mom said, "I told G Kitty they didn't have to come tomorrow and invited them to the party here instead. Is that okay?"

I nodded, trying not to be glum about the whole thing. Mom glanced at the list I had open.

Quinn's New Year's Resolutions

#1 Help mom stay healthy.

#2 Drive a car before any of my friends. I am not kidding. Otherwise I will ONCE AGAIN be last since all my friends will turn 15 before I do. I just want to be first, at one thing that is important, for once.

#3 Make an unhealthy meal that Grandma Kitty says tastes delicious.

#4 Get kissed by a boy. Not Tucker.

"I failed at number one, didn't I?" I asked. "The

doctor said I had helped, but I didn't."

"You helped tremendously," Mom said. "I could face everything with courage because of you. My moods were always up because of you. My life has purpose and meaning because of you and Tucker and Dad. And God."

"I've been hoping that number four might happen on Valentine's Day," I said. "I guess not now."

"Well, you'd better not tell your dad that you're hoping to kiss anyone before your wedding day, or he's going to lock you in the house for the rest of your life," Mom said. She kissed me on the forehead. "There's always something good just around the corner."

I looked at the purse again after she'd left. I didn't open it. I wouldn't. I pulled out my mom's list—which neither of us had mentioned—and read through it.

Mary's List of Things to Do Before I Die
(in 80 years that is)

#1 Fly a plane
#2 ~~Kiss a boy~~
#3 ~~Bake homemade bread~~
#4 Dance the Hustle (okay, I know disco is out, but still)
#5 ~~Start my own business~~
#6 ~~Have a daughter~~

Dad was learning the Hustle. Mom and Tucker would go to Boeing Field tomorrow and sign up for flight lessons. One thing left—maybe—and it was a surprise. The dress.

Later that night I tiptoed to the computer to see if anyone had responded to my email. I needed encouragement! I got an email from Adam.

I'm really sorry you won't be here Tuesday night. It won't be the same without you. I have something for you, something I wanted to give to you on Valentine's Day. I'm going to overnight it with FedEx on Monday after I talk with some of the others. Don't open it till just before the party. Promise?

Adam

CHAPTER TWELVE

When we woke up on Tuesday, Valentine's Day, the sun was out. I knew the day would hold some surprises; I just didn't know how many there would actually be.

Dad was making breakfast.

"Pancakes?" I asked.

"Well, since I only know how to grill steaks, make chili, or flip flapjacks, I figured pancakes were the best option of the three," he teased.

"Yeah," I said. "Good choice." I noticed he had dropped the batter into little heart shapes, which was pretty good for a guy to do, if you asked me. I popped a chocolate peanut butter heart into my mouth to tide me over till he served them up.

Mom sat down at the table. "How pretty!" she said. Tucker poured some raspberry syrup over the pancakes, and just as he did, we heard a knock at the door.

I opened it. It was Annie.

"Ready for school?" she asked. I nodded. I wanted to go one last day and say good-bye to everyone.

"Here," she said and handed a box to me. "I'll see you there in a few minutes."

The only box I was expecting today was one from Adam. It hadn't arrived yet. So this was a nice surprise!

I went into my room and opened it up. My shirt! The shirt she said she wasn't going to be able to finish. I tried it on. It fit perfectly. It really made my eyes and skin color look pretty. I pulled my hair back loosely in some of the leftover satin ribbon she had left in the box and went out to the living room.

"I don't know where you're going dressed like that, Tiger Lily," Dad said. "But the first boy who makes you an offer of marriage is going to have to talk with me."

"No worries, Dad," Tucker said. "Never happen."

I threw a pillow at him.

We walked to our last day at Fitzschool, but it

didn't really seem sad, because I knew we'd see everyone later that night at the party. More than one hundred people were coming, and the party was the buzz of the school day. Even I was excited now!

It did feel a little sad to pack up my books and my desk. Neither Annie nor I would be back here tomorrow.

No one asked if Mom's treatment worked. They all knew better, and I was glad for that because I didn't want the day spoiled in any way.

After school Annie and I met in the rec room to finish setting up.

"Thanks again for the shirt," I said. I had taken it off so that I wouldn't get it dirty before tonight. "It is the most wonderful gift a friend has ever given me, and I will never forget you. But how did you ever do it?"

Annie started unfolding the tablecloths as she talked. "At first I thought I was going to have way enough time, because I was stuck in the apartment when my mom was sick. So I worked on your shirt way back then, thinking I would have enough time to do the dress, too."

She set a glass bowl of water in the middle of the table and looked at me questioningly. I nodded my approval and floated a single rose in the water. We moved on to the next table. I had already supervised the receipt of the linens and flowers yesterday, paid for by the volunteer committee but supervised by me. I had ended up doing the flowers anyway. Not in Leavenworth, but here.

"So then when I got sick I was in a complete panic," Annie continued, "because I knew I shouldn't have spent the time doing your shirt and now I wasn't going to be able to finish your mom's dress."

She quickly looked over her shoulder to make sure my mom hadn't crept down or something.

"Is the dress done?" Annie asked me. "Was your grandma able to finish it up for you?"

I shrugged my shoulders. "I don't know. I don't think so. If it were good news, I think G Kitty would have told me. I don't think I can deal with any more bad news right now, so I'm just not dealing with it at all."

Annie nodded. "Is your grandma coming down for the party?"

I nodded back. "So we'll see if the dress is done when she gets here. In the meantime, Mom knows nothing and has picked out a white dress, which will look pretty with a red rose."

We finished the tablecloths and the centerpieces. There was a place in the front of the room for the musicians. The volunteers had contacted a local string quartet and asked them to donate their talent—and they had agreed! Even the Valentine's party at home wouldn't have a string quartet. I wondered if a string quartet could play music for the Hustle.

The inflated balloons arrived—the one detail I had left for today. "Do you want to set the balloons in the corner or at each table?" Annie asked. She sat down for a minute and rested even though she'd been helping only a little.

"Wherever you want," I said, keeping my eye on the Anderson House door. Where was the FedEx driver? "It's your party now."

She put her hand on my arm. "No, Quinn, it's your party. You did it all."

"I did it all for *you*!" I said. Then, before things got too serious I popped a balloon, and we both laughed when the doorman jumped up.

We set tables in the back for food, which would be cooked by the Fitz Cancer Center volunteer staff. They had really gone all out to help us make this party a success. I think they sensed how important it was to the residents—and to Annie in particular.

The UPS man was here! Maybe Adam had sent it by UPS instead.

The doorman was signaling to me.

"Here," he said. "Can you bring this up to your dad?"

My *dad*? The package was sent from Chicago. It wasn't from Adam.

"Be right back," I said to Annie and ran the package upstairs. "Dad!" I called once I reached the apartment. "There's a package here for you."

"Oh good," he said. He looked at the box. My mom and Tucker and I looked at him.

"What *is* it?" Mom asked.

"That's for me to know and you to find out," Dad said. "I'm bringing this to Gunther's."

So now Annie's dad was in on a secret?

I ran back downstairs and made sure the rec room looked okay. It was almost time to get ourselves ready for the party.

Annie and I put our arms around each other. "It looks good, doesn't it?" she asked.

The bowls in the centers of the tables shimmered, and the roses wafted a beautiful scent over the tables. The balloons sparkled and glimmered in the corner of the room. The musicians started arriving and warming up. The volunteers started to set out the buffet.

"It looks great," I said. "I'd better go upstairs and get ready."

As I did, I caught a glimpse of the FedEx man approaching the door. "It's FedEx!" I said.

Annie looked at me strangely, and I realized I hadn't told her about Adam's email. "I'll tell you later," I said, eager to get the box.

Sure enough, it was for me. As soon as I got to the

apartment, I kicked Tucker out of our room.

I opened the box. First I drew out a small pouch of flower petals. There was a note in it.

Dear Quinn,

Thanks for letting me do the flowers since you couldn't be here. It was really generous of you because I feel like I belong now that I have a job. I know this was supposed to be really special to you, so I will make sure that it goes really great and tell you all about it.

Your new friend,
Michelle

That was really sweet. I was so glad I had let her take over the flowers. She didn't sound like a boy-poacher to me, either.

The next packet I drew out of the box was an envelope from Holly. I opened it up.

Dear Q,

I am sorry you won't be here but I kind of figured you wouldn't come back. Why? Because I know the kind of friend you are. If Annie needed you there, you'd stay. I'm glad you're that kind of friend to me. I hope you have no plans on Friday night. Sleepover at my house. After this:

She'd attached an invitation.

Please Come
What? Homecoming party for Quinn
Where? Holly's house
When? Friday night
Bring candy! Pizza served

How fun. A party for *me*!

I'd keep my new shirt nice and clean. Sophisticated looking. I could wear it on Friday.

Next I took out a big bag of . . . Moose Munch! It had a ribbon around the top and a tag attached. "To Annie From Your Friends."

I smiled. I'd put it at her place at the table.

There was a knock on the door. "Quinn?"

It was Mom.

"Just a second," I said. I reached back into the box for the one remaining item. It was wrapped in pretty red paper and a small card was attached. I opened the card. It read, "Quinn, you always were good at symbolism, so I know you'll get this. See you soon. Adam."

I peeled the wrapping paper off to find one perfect, large Hershey's Kiss.

I knew what he meant.

I hid it under the wrapping paper. "You can come in now," I called out to my mom.

She came in looking so pretty in her white dress. "What'd you get?"

I showed her everything except the Kiss. She found it anyway.

"Who is this from?"

"Adam."

Mom smiled. "Where's your list?"

"What list?" I was confused.

"Your New Year's resolutions," she said.

"In the drawer." She signaled for me to go and get it, so I did.

She took a pencil and drew a line through number four.

"But that's *not* what I meant!" I said.

"See? Something to make both you *and* Dad happy."

We sat cross-legged on my bed and laughed together.

I heard a knock at the door. It was G Kitty and Grandpa Doug! "I'll get it," I said. When I opened the door, G Kitty carried the cardboard under-the-bed box that Annie had given her with the fabric. I knew what was inside.

She handed it to me. "Here, you give it to her."

"Nope," I shook my head. "*We* will do it."

G Kitty and I drew my mom into her bedroom. "We have a surprise for you," I said.

Mom looked genuinely surprised. "What is it?"

"Open the box, dear," G Kitty said.

We three sat on the bed and Mom lifted the lid from the cardboard box. "Oh, oh my," she said, breathing out slowly. She lifted the dress from the shoulders and held it up. "It's a perfect match. It's exactly like the doll dress. Chic, subtle, fashionable."

Tears sprang into her eyes, and she held it up in front of her and looked in the mirror. I have to admit, with her dark hair and shiny nails it looked stunning.

She turned around and hugged us, first me, then G Kitty. "It's perfect. I can't imagine a more wonderful gift today."

"Try it on!" G Kitty urged her. Mom slipped out of her white dress and slipped on the red velvet dress. It hung just perfectly on her. She got a pair of black shoes out of the bag she'd already packed to go home and slipped them on. When she turned to face us, the bottom of the dress twirled and flounced.

"You'll be the most beautiful person there," I told her.

Surprisingly, she nodded her agreement. "I don't know how I couldn't be, in this dress."

G Kitty's hands trembled. "Better late than never?"

Mom put Grandma's face between her hands and kissed each cheek. "Never a better time than right now," she said.

Mom went into the living room, where Dad whistled and Tucker clapped. G Kitty pulled me aside. "If you'd gone home on Sunday, I wouldn't have finished. Your staying here an extra couple of days allowed me to get it done—and get it perfect."

Maybe God *had* arranged everything just so, for Annie and me both.

We went down to the party and ate and danced. Tucker showed everyone his card tricks and even let Frankie show Hotel, Motel to the crowd. After about an hour Dad signaled to Mr. Meyer, who set a disco ball in the center of the dance floor. *That* was what had been in the box Dad had rushed to him! All at once the quartet started playing disco music for the Hustle, and Dad escorted Mom onto the floor.

"You're kidding!" she said to him as they left.

"You'll wish I was kidding when you see how lame I dance," Dad said. "But I had to try for you."

He looked so funny out there, like a diseased chicken, really, but I didn't tell him that. I just looked at the love he had for my mom and my mom had for him.

After that they played a slow dance, and I saw Annie's dad kiss Annie's mom as they twirled onto the floor.

Annie wiped away a tear. It was perfect.

I ran upstairs to take a bathroom break, and then I

grabbed my lip gloss from my bedroom drawer. As I did, I caught a glimpse of my journal with my lists.

I whipped out a pencil.

Coffee drinks—done!

Quinn's List of Drinks I Must Have While
in Seattle, Before My Starbucks Card
Runs Out of Credit

#1 ~~Hazelnut white chocolate mocha with extra whipped cream~~

#2 ~~Green Tazo tea with two packs of raw sugar~~

#3 ~~Chantico Drinking Chocolate~~

#4 ~~Double espresso. Straight up.~~

Card tricks—done!

Four Tricks to Teach Tucker
Before Valentine's Day

#1 ~~All the Aces~~

#2 ~~Hotel and Motel~~

#3 ~~Order, Please~~

#4 ~~Vanishing Card~~

Mom's stuff—done! And even one that wasn't on there. The dress!

Mary's List of Things to Do Before I Die
(in 80 years that is)

#1 ~~Fly a plane~~
#2 ~~Kiss a boy~~
#3 ~~Bake homemade bread~~
#4 ~~Dance the Hustle (okay, I know disco is out,~~
~~but still)~~
#5 ~~Start my own business~~
#6 ~~Have a daughter~~

My New Year's Resolutions—done in time for Mom to see them all! Except number four was a little unfair if you ask me.

Quinn's New Year's Resolutions
#1 ~~Help mom stay healthy.~~
#2 ~~Drive a car before any of my friends. I~~
~~am not kidding. Otherwise I will ONCE~~
~~AGAIN be last since all my friends will~~
~~turn 15 before I do. I just want to be~~
~~first, at one thing that is important, for~~
~~once.~~
#3 ~~make an unhealthy meal that Grandma~~
~~Kitty says tastes delicious.~~
#4 ~~Get kissed by a boy. Not Tucker.~~

Only Annie's list bugged me. I had no idea, really,

about number 3. I wished somehow, some way, I would know for sure. Because then I'd know she could deal with it whether the cancer came back or not.

Things I Will Pray for Annie
#1 ~~That she will find Jesus waiting for her~~
#2 ~~That she will meet Sun-Hea~~
#3 That she will make peace with her mom having cancer
#4 ~~That her parents will fall in love again~~

I went back downstairs. Annie came to the table. "This is great." She held out a handful of Moose Munch. "Your church is so cool."

"It's not my church," I said. "It's God's. And yours, too. But I'll bet you find a good one in Olathe, too."

Annie smiled and headed back to her table, where she sat between her happy mom and dad. Ben's family was at the same table, of course. I had the feeling those two would keep in touch.

I rubbed my mom's shoulders; she looked tired. "Do you want to go?" I asked.

"Yes," she nodded, fingering the trim on her dress with love. "It's been wonderful, but I've never been one to argue when it's time to go home."

My eyes filled with tears, and I hugged her as the strings played like angel harps behind us.

We both knew what she meant.

ONE YEAR LATER

When Dad pulled into the driveway at our house in Leavenworth, Annie jumped out before the car was stopped. "I feel just like I'm coming back to my second home!" she said.

"You're going to feel like you're coming back to get your broken legs set in casts if you're not careful about the ice," I teased her.

She looked so good. Older. I suppose I did, too, even though it didn't seem like it. I wasn't a pre-freshman anymore. I was a real one. Actually, I was a pre-sophomore.

"So how is your church?" I asked as we lugged her suitcase upstairs.

"Good. No boys as cute as Ben, and no Moose Munch. But lots of good stuff," she said. "The strangest thing. Sometimes when I'm there I catch a whiff of your perfume from someplace—Tiger Lily. My parents still don't come, but my mom is interested in the luncheon next month. I'm praying for them. She sometimes reads the Bible your mom gave her."

"I'm so glad," I said. "Thanks for telling me that."

When we got to my room, she unzipped her suitcase and took out a big picture frame. "Here we are."

I looked at the two girls, just a few years apart. Sisters at last. "Did you have a good time when she was here?"

"Totally. And my mom was fine with it. Enjoyed herself, actually."

"She and your dad?"

"Seeing a counselor," Annie said. "But things are good. Better. They *date,* even though I'm not allowed to yet."

I laughed with her.

She pointed to the stack of diaries on the corner of my desk. "Have you read them yet?"

I looked at them, the dates neatly written in Mom's handwriting on the masking tape on the covers. "No. I will, though. Maybe this summer. I'm just not ready to 'hear' her voice yet."

Annie nodded understandingly. "What time do we have to be there?" she asked.

"Soon. Are you ready with the prayer?"

"Ready as I'll ever be."

I sat down and she braided my hair, and then I pulled hers back in a ponytail. We each put on a Norwegian stocking cap. "Remember how nervous I was last year?" I asked.

"No," she reminded me. "I couldn't go."

Not *wouldn't*. Couldn't.

"But you're not only going this year; you're leading the prayer."

"It's an important cause. My mom had breast cancer. I'm personally involved," she said. "I'm proud to be the pray-er for the second annual Ribbons in the Snow fund-raiser."

I made a mental note to cross off the remaining thing on Annie's list.

Things I Will Pray for Annie
#1 That she will find Jesus waiting for her
#2 That she will meet Sun-Hea
#3 That she will make peace with her mom having cancer
#4 That her parents will fall in love again

We checked our look in the mirror over my dresser. She saw the tiny red velvet bag there. She reached over and touched the outside.

"I remember this," she said. "And what you told me your mom said."

"To open it after she'd gone," I said.

"Did you?" Annie asked.

"Yeah. About a week later when I could bring myself to do it."

Annie stroked the fabric. She would never ask me, but I wanted to offer. I hadn't shown any of my other friends, not even Holly, who was still my best friend. But Annie and I had been through something that no one else I knew had. I knew she'd understand.

"Do you want to see what's inside?" I asked her.

She nodded. I picked up the purse and dumped it into her hand. Two conversation hearts fell out.

She arranged them. *I Luv U* and *C U Soon*.

She nodded. "You'll see her again."

"I know I will," I said. "At the chocolate table." I smiled. "Ready to go?"

"Ready." She fixed her cap and we walked out of the door arm in arm.

*If your first concern is to look after yourself,
you'll never find yourself. But if you forget
about yourself and look to me,
you'll find both yourself and me.*

Matthew 10:39 THE MESSAGE

Connect with other FRIENDS FOR A SEASON readers at *www.FriendsforaSeason.com*!

- Sign up for Sandra Byrd's newsletter
- Send e-cards to your friends
- Download FRIENDS FOR A SEASON wallpapers and icons
- Get a sneak peek at upcoming books in the series
- Learn more about the places and events featured in each book

www.FriendsforaSeason.com

WANT *MORE?*

Read About the Other Girls in the
FRIENDS FOR A SEASON Series

ISLAND GIRL

Meg is excited to return to her grand-parents' island home like she does each summer. But this summer everything is different—Meg's mother is remarried with a new baby on the way, and now a new girl has taken her place at her grandparents' berry farm. Can Meg find her place in a con-stantly changing family and figure out what life, family, and friendship are all about?
FRIENDS FOR A SEASON #1

CHOPSTICK

Paige wants more attention from her family. Kate wants her family to stand out a little less. Winning a local song-writing contest will give each girl the boost she needs. There's only one catch—the girls didn't count on becoming friends. Paige and Kate learn about faith and worship and winning at all costs.
FRIENDS FOR A SEASON #2

Learn more about the girls of the FRIENDS FOR A SEASON books at *www.friendsforaseason.com!*

Look for the 4th FRIENDS FOR A SEASON book
Daisy Chains, coming March 2006!

◊ BETHANYHOUSE